For Carol, Roger, and Richard. Three people who should
be here to see this.

Front cover image by the author with thanks to the Binge's

Author image by Myk G

The Hunter, the Hunted and the Prey

Prologue: The before time

Deep in the heart of the English countryside, close enough to Derby to be called local, the grade two-listed building of the Ellinworth family stood. Inside the low stone wall lay a hundred acres of tendered forest, deer and one of the biggest ornate gardens in the area. The Ellinworth's were one of the few titled families to survive, keeping themselves not only supported, but also affluent through clever business and land transactions. Lord Ellinworth was widely considered one of the best businessmen in England, growing his already comfortable fortune into a massive empire. His wife, the Lady Ellinworth, was described as a natural beauty; her image in the glossy women's magazines compared her to Lady Diana. They kept their extensive manor well maintained, well staffed, and private. Their lives may be in the public eye, but only the part they showed. They had no scandal, no insider news, and no reputation, save generosity and success. Then disaster struck a cruel blow. On returning from a skiing trip to the Alps their private jet, flown by His Lordship, ran into difficulties and crashed into the snowy emptiness. When the rescue team arrived they found the couple frozen in an eternal embrace in the wreck of the plane. The title passed down to their only son, and shares in the estate dropped by nearly half. Frederick was a drifter, a loner, and a lazy waste of space. All the staff felt double the grief at the loss of their master. They knew it was the end.

It was early one afternoon when the newly titled Lord Ellinworth rolled out of his bed to the midday sun. Hopdyke, the head butler, glided silently in and placed the solid silver tray beside the bed. On it was a bone china plate with a toast rack and fresh orange juice, and an 'urgent' memo from accounts. Lord Ellinworth or Elphy as his few friends knew him, groaned at the sight of the mound of paper and rolled away. "Bloody paperwork," he moaned. Hopdyke kept his plain, professional expression as he surveyed his late master's main bedchamber. A tear formed in the corner of his eye, not only of grief for the accident two months passed, but of the changes he now saw. Turning noiselessly Hopdyke floated away, feeling anger and despair. He loathed his new master, but also pitied him. There would be a bad end to the young man, he knew it.

Lying on his back Elphy once again tried to go back to sleep. That dammed memo. He had earned, through the accident on the family jet, a ridiculous fortune and now was being told that unless he invested a large enough portion, the money would be passed to the board of directors. Elphy would get an 'income' from them, non negotiable. His father, ever the businessman, had insured his life, and his family, for a massive sum, and on his death it was paid into the family account. Now that had passed to the only family member left; his son. Elphy had ignored the memo since the accident, getting drunk and partying all over the world in a 'fluid wake' for his parents; neither had he got along with too well. Elphy was a dreamer, a drifter, and, if he was honest, a drunk. His head still spun from celebrating the start of 2018, two days ago. The help had naturally cleaned his elegant Georgian bedchambers, even his vomit stains on the three hundred year old carpeting, and the small scratches from the last filly he had bedded on the four-poster he slept in. There was a yellow stain on the historic printed wallpaper, but Elphy hated that too. All he wanted was to have fun. Years of boring private school had killed joy for him. Now he was getting back all he could.

Groaning he crawled out of bed, on the rough carpet to the over decorated bathroom. After draining a gallon of something from his bladder young Elphy groaned back to bed. His phone flashed a warning about the full message box. That damned memo! What to spend that money on? He could, and had blown thousands of pounds on booze and women, and sometimes drugs too, but how to blow five billion was beyond him. Couldn't be charity, a popular fraud for tax dodgers. Couldn't be sent overseas. Had to be in a physical company he didn't own. England had just been finally released from the common market and that had sent shock waves over the world. The stock markets were in turmoil, with the Euro struggling, European economy failing and wars the only thing on the up. Elphy loathed weapons, even removing his father's collection of antique shotguns. So what to do?

As he always did when faced with a choice Elphy turned on the television. It never ceased to astound him how often that came up with the answers. As usual it did not let him down. BBC News 24 was the default channel for his father; the TV automatically picked it first. Headline news, fresh off the press with the ink still wet, was the breakthrough in DNA extraction. Some Norwegian scientist it seemed had managed to find a way to work out a DNA code from only a fragment. Something to do with a gene in DNA that was the defining gene for each species. With funding, he said, any fossilised animal could be recreated. Elphy looked over the TV to the one shelf that was truly his. On it were a few tatty magazines of naked girls, blurred images from blurred nights out, and a stuffed dinosaur he'd had as a child. He rolled onto the floor and swung a wild arm, knocking it to the floor. Trying to focus he held it in both hands like an old man trying to use a smart phone. The toy was originally light blue, a gift from a summer theme park trip, one of the last times he was happy, before being packed off to boarding school and forgotten. It represented the past, the good times, now nearly twenty years old. It hadn't had an easy life, but neither had he. Dog-eared and missing an eye it certainly needed some magic to revive it. Maybe the Norwegian doctor had the right idea? Be a good waste of money, just what he needed. With a ghost of a smile despite the hangover Elphy picked up his cell phone and dialled.

Doctor Arvid Dokken was a happy man. With the massive funding from the Ellinworth Estate he had finally achieved his dream. Soon fame would be his. In an old opencast mine in the English Lake District they had built a massive semi underground laboratory. Some called it Blofeld s den after the James Bond villain. It certainly fitted. The lab buildings and accommodation were on the surface, powered by a massive bank of solar panels. Underneath, half hidden by rubble to disguise them, were the animal pens. These massive caverns had their own mini ecosystem, with UV lights, plants, trees, even rivers. Everything a prehistoric creature would need. Today they would finally be used. In the main egg lab the first shell cracked, and a pointed snout poked through the simulated egg. There was a bubbling of soft cheers, kept quiet so as not to disturb the baby, and assistants dressed in tatters of cloth to hide their outlines helped the creatures emerge. This was a good day for Dokken; soon he could report his findings.

He was more than a little concerned his employer had

insisted on secrecy, and the underground lab. They could have succeeded just as easily on the surface, without the need for expensive underground pens, but the young man had been insistent. Some joked he wanted to spend money, others said it was for a secret game reserve where you could hunt animals without fear of media attack. That worried Dokken, fearing his masterpiece could become a rich man's quarry. Pushing the fears back he concentrated on the readings from the other egg batches. Likening himself to Henry Wu from the old 1990's film Dokken knew he was doing the incredible, but also knew there was a big margin for error. As long as everything went smooth, he would be fine. They would be fine.

The stock market crash of 2025 was staggering. Overnight the bottom literally dropped from the financial world. Companies floating in the seas of economy were now sucked to the bottom by a credit crunch Kraken. Even the World Bank fell, leaving nowhere for companies, and even countries to turn. Riots started, small, but grew fast. Riots turned to gang warfare, then the powers fell and war was declared. Never on paper, but the world fought for its survival like two starving dogs over the last steak. With no control the fate of mankind looked sealed. The only saving grace was that when the heads of governments fell, so too did the control of the planets nuclear arsenal. With the nukes neutralised traditional warfare took over. Gangs grew in power until they ran cities, then counties, then regions, and finally countries. Land was burned to make it useless to their enemies, buildings pillaged for valuables, women pillaged for a brief relief.

As the wars continued, nobody noticed the holding area deep in the scenic lake district of England. The semi secret laboratory funded by the late Lord Ellinworth, who died trying to defend his manor house from a gang of thieves, went unnoticed by the hoarders and fighters. The staff hid there as long as they dared before risking a breakout to the nearby military depot, only a few miles away. They didn't make it. The winter fell; cold after the mild summer, and a heavy snowstorm trapped and froze them. Their creations, still in their pens, waited for feeding time, until the solar panels under a small avalanche of snow, gave out and power was lost. The pens clicked open, the contents released. Outside, while the fires still burned, the people still fought, long dead recreations explored the new menu available.

Chapter One

Through the beige grass a lone goat tried to nibble a mouthful. It stopped occasionally to sniff the breeze and scan for danger. Two more of it's herd grazed nearby.

All was quiet, with the brisk wind in the dry grass, blowing the warm sun away from the parched ground. It had been a very hot summer. Wells had dried, livestock died, people starved. The three goats continued nibbling the stunted shoots. Nearby was the low mud wall of a village. The mud was cracked, but still a foot thick, with a step along the inside wide enough for a man to walk below the lip of the wall. Patches showed darker areas where the wall had been repaired.

The wind changed and the goats all paused, sniffing and looking. They were in the open, a fair distance from a small wood of pine and oak trees. Sensing no danger they resumed eating. They didn't look up when the low rumble was carried past on the wind. Then the snapping of a branch. The goats again looked around, but saw nothing. By now it was too late. Standing still on the edge of the woods the predator slowly opened its jaws and charged. In five seconds it was amongst the goats, ducking its head and flicking one goat high in the air before going for the second. The other two had fled together, making the hairless biped's job much easier. Once more the head went down, and came up blooded. Three carcases lay on the grass, dark blood soaking into the dry soil. As the creature paused to look for threats it missed the small figure that stood up from the very ground, aim a tube at it, and fired. Smoke billowed and something flashed towards the predator. When it hit it exploded with an almighty boom that echoed off the walls. The decapitated body tried to stand but devoid of instructions it finally toppled and fell.

Men in animal skins and cloth rags, ran whooping and cheering from the village, most running to the meat, some to the man. There would be rich eating for months now. The man himself simply shouldered the tube, dusted the soil in which he had hidden away, and walked into the village. His name was Christopher Spencer, as best he knew. He was a loner, a cast out, a wanderer. But he was also a Hunter. And now he was going to get paid.

"I can't thank you enough," said elder Hartley. "To rid us of that thing, and all this meat! Truly a great gift you have given us."

Spencer smiled as best he could amidst the dancing throng of villagers. The sun had set, giving blessed relief from the heat of the day. The men danced their dance around a large bonfire while the women cut and prepared the meat from the kill. Some pretty young ladies looked at Chris with more than joy, eyeing his tattered and patched clothes made from real cloth, his scuffed black boots, and his shaven face. He knew they would want to express their gratitude their own way, but he had little time for that.

"Sorry?" Chris hadn't realised Hartley had spoken to him.

"I asked if you could stay awhile. You have helped us so much we want to return the favour."

"Thanks," replied Chris, "but I'm needed elsewhere. I shall stay tonight and tomorrow I think. A chance to stretch my legs and let the young 'un see the sights."

Both men turned to see Marty Fritz Herbert, already surrounded by young women, recounting his rapt audience with tales of heroism and daring. Chris smiled. He knew Marty wouldn't want to leave too early, and to force him would only result in him sulking for a few days. Anyway, Chris needed time to sort a few problems, and the meat that was his reward would take some time to cure.

Politely excusing himself from the party, and shaking off Hartley with some struggle, Chris headed back to his space. He never slept in a hut, or even a house if the village was large enough to own one. He preferred sleeping in the one place he felt safe. His car.

It was pure luck, even Chris had to admit that, the discovery made by the young Chris Spencer on that hot, still day. Drifting through a thick forest hunting for food he fell through a hole into a massive underground shelter. After some exploring he found heaps of clothes, weapons, armour, food and equipment. Even some vehicles remained. It was one of the military storehouses, made ready for a war they couldn't fight against. It took Chris only days to figure out, fix and use all he needed. Once he had a vehicle, weapons, clothes, equipment and a safe place to call home he was ready. The car he finally settled on was an old army Land Rover, stripped down and with mounts all over for guns. Finding there was loads of fuel stored in underground tanks he prepared the car for his needs. Now he lived in it, slept in it, and worked from it. On the back was the rocket launcher he had used, reloaded, cleaned and ready for use.

Chris swung himself into the driver's seat and groped in the dashboard. Finally he pulled out a crumpled notebook and pencil. With his tongue out of one side Chris carefully wrote: one Allosaurus, head kill, RPG. This was written below the long list of other kills, what, where, how. Chris knew he was possibly the only person who knew about these things, having found a laboratory near his base, complete with paper books on the different species, what was known and what the scientists had learnt. It also made it easier to kill them. Chris' reputation had spread, either by the words of locals, or the armoured convoys passing by taking supplies to the big cities. The city inhabitants hated outsiders like Chris, and he was happy with that. He hated the soft, flabby city dwellers.

Using a nearby tree Chris unhooked his hammock from the side of the car and hung it from a low branch.

The noise from the party still roared, and the light from the fire cast crazy shadows on the hut walls. Chris was asleep within minutes though. Around him were people he could trust, and thick walls should the people fail him. He was safe, so he could sleep.

Two days later Marty threw the last string of cured meat in the back of the car. His face said it all, and was reflected in the faces of his group of admirers. As always after a kill there was the pure joy of a job done, the pressure lifted and a chance to relax and unwind. If nubile young ladies wanted to throw themselves on him Marty didn't mind. It cured, or caused, the itch. Chris as always still worked on like there was no rewards, no bonuses. He never took opportunities for fun. Stale as old meat was Chris, but bloody good at his job.

"What you moping about for now?" Chris asked, breaking Marty from his revelry.

"Nuthin'," he replied. "Where to next, boss?"

"Not sure yet. Got a whisper of something lurking around down southwards. Maybe something nasty, probably not though. Still, gotta go look"

Chris checked the truck one last time before dropping onto the seat, which coughed out a small cloud of dust. Marty flopped into his, automatically checking the belt feed of ammunition to the small machine gun mounted in front of him. He still looked unhappy.

"If there isn't anything to go for why not stay here? Safe, comfy and we don't need nuthin' soon."

"Because if we stay here we'll get too comfy, and those girls you spent the night with will be asking for their babies dad." Chris shot Marty a brief smile, then turned the key. A diesel engine was rare in these days, even with the big long smoking road trains that passed sometimes. Half the villagers jumped at the noise, children cried and mothers held them closer. When the black cloud had cleared Chris and Marty were almost out of earshot, Marty still waving cheerfully.

"You always ask that, don't you?" Chris said as they passed the spot of the kill, still red with blood and black with flies.

"Meh," replied Marty.

Chris had no idea how old the boy was, or how old he was to be honest. Both were orphaned, both were lost, both were found. Chris had found him after a village was decimated by something. He was the only survivor in a hut, hidden by his mother. It could have been men who attacked, it could have been an animal. All they left was a scared teenager. That was three years ago, and Marty still acted like a kid.

"Well, it wouldn't have worked anyway. Can't see you being tied to just one group of girls," Chris joked.

Marty smiled. "Imagine trying to remember all their names!"

Chris laughed, both at the joke and relief. Leaving a village was always tough. Heading out alone from the walls of safety.

"Uh oh," Marty warned. "Trouble on the horizon."

Chris slowed the car, looking ahead at the dust cloud. There had been strong winds and dust storms recently, the kind that would ruin the meat in the back. But this was smaller, and localised. That meant either a roaming band of men looking for women and food, or a convoy. Black smoke mingled with the dust. Convoy.

Even though the drivers hated outsiders, being allowed to live in the poorest parts of the big cities, Chris drove forwards to join them. As the big long trucks rumbled by, each covered in metal plating and painted black, Chris matched speeds with the lead lorry and shouted over the din.

"Greetings! Any news from up north?"

"Go away, scum!" a voice shouted from inside. "I got a guy with a rifle looking at your nut and one hand touches metal you won't have a place to hang a hat from!"

Chris smiled as charmingly as he could. "I was only asking if you had news. I'm not here for what you have. Just news then I will go on my own way."

The driver, hidden in the depths of his cab stuck a tanned arm through the plating and threw a paper roll out. The wind whipped it away, spiralling into the dust cloud.

"Many thanks friend," called Chris. The hand waved back a less friendly gesture, and Chris slowed to collect the paper.

Looking over his shoulder Marty tried to read the print. These 'newspapers' were rare, brief and usually old. This one seemed newer, with less creases and stains than normal. Also it had a date stamp which was rare. On the front of the four page roll was the main updates. Later came messages from companies about trade values and goods. The last page was convoy information, and warnings of raiding parties, missing people and road conditions. It was to this Chris turned first. Scanning quickly through the rough print Chris grunted then passed the roll back to Marty. As he read the front page Marty traced a finger along the lines. His reading was improving, but still a little slow. Chris had to teach himself to read, then teach Marty when he found him. It would help if Marty was able to concentrate more on what he was doing.

Chris drove down the dirt road away from the convoy.

They were headed to the big city nearby and he wanted nothing to do with them. They lived in a little bubble of luxury, making trinkets they swapped for food and things. Soft, fat people in soft, fat houses living a soft, fat life. The only danger they faced was getting up in the morning. Chris let Marty finish the paper in silence, knowing any distraction would slow his reading more. The back page had reported some disturbance near them, but that was probably the Allosaurus they had just killed. He planned instead to loop westwards and then south to avoid the major settlements scattered around.

There was one abandoned place that was too small to be a village, yet still had walls. Maybe it was built in the before, but was useless now so was left alone. This suited Chris. It was far enough away to be ignored, but close enough to be a storehouse for him. Inside was more cured meat, a well of clean drinking water, thick stone like walls and a roof. It was secure, easily defended and protected. There he stored ammunition for his southern trips, equipment and supplies. It made a perfect staging post for him, saving wasted time and fuel heading back north to his underground bunker.

It was hidden in a small stand of trees, hard to find from the outside. As usual Chris drove around it in a wide circle to check for signs of recent activity. Seeing none he went to a dry riverbed that ran through the trees, hiding his tracks. Finally they saw the low, boxy building ahead, the rusting shutter door one side. Chris parked beside the door, and waited for Marty to finish his paper.

"Done?" Chris asked.

Marty tossed the paper in the back. "Yep. Not much there, just usual crap."

"Good. What there is to talk about these days is beyond me. Why even bother?"

Marty helped Chris open the roller door. It screeched a little, but Chris had repaired it well and it took seconds to roll it up. Instinctively they both drew pistols from hip holsters and checked the building. Once cleared they began unloading the car, refilling fuel and ammunition, and storing the meat.

"You think they have better papers in the cities?" Marty asked while they hung the meat in the far end of the bunker.

"Probably, or have some slave read it to them."

"Wonder what they looks like," Marty said.

"Probably still better dressed than we are," Chris replied.

"Who?"

"The slaves," Chris said, and heaved the last of the meat onto a hook suspended from the ceiling. He then drove the car inside, shut the door and joined Marty on the flat roof, keeping a watchful eye on the trees. Marty was already in his hammock rereading the paper he had retrieved from the car.

"I meant the papers. This is old paper, remade. Feel how stiff it is. Bet they have new paper there."

"Why do you care?" Chris asked, sitting on his own hammock and laying a low table with rifle parts to clean.

"Well, you know? Just wonderin', that's all."

Chris knew when Marty went defensive. Usually about women, or alcohol if a village managed to brew any. He tried to cover his past, or lack of. With no memory of his life before Chris found him he was always insecure.

Chris started cleaning a rifle bolt with a rag. "Maybe we'll see one day."

"Yeah right," Marty said. "You hate living in a village. You'd hate a city, like, a lot more. Too much comfort."

"Not really. Gotta think of the future. Maybe earn some coin, get a big fancy house, with an upstairs. Live like the rich do."

Marty laughed. "You could run as mayor. Mayor Spencer. Have one of those furry cloaks and big gold chains.

Chris was laughing too. He stood, waved the rifle bolt like a sword and strutted. Marty knelt before him, to be knighted.

"I dub you Sire Fritz Herbert, of the Order of the Bolt," Chris said, tapping Marty on the shoulder. He then dropped back on his hammock leaving Marty still on the floor, his knighted shoulders rocking in laughter.

"Really though," Chris said, returning to his cleaning, "me in a city? Not what you call high society. They have fancy clothes and healthy skin."

"No rips either," Marty said from the floor, fingering a small tear in his shirt.

"No rips. Want to live in a world of no rips?" Chris asked.

"Maybe, but I doubt it. Need to have a bath then." Marty plucked a bolt carrier from the pile and absently rubbed it with a rag.

"You still do," said Chris.

"Had one a few months ago," said Marty.

"That was a flood, and you only got half wet," replied Chris.

"Good enough for me."

Chris smiled and they both silently went about cleaning and oiling the rifle. Once together Chris sat on his chair near the edge of the flat roof looking out while Marty snored gently. The sun had set, leaving a gentle breeze through the arid trees. Chris liked this time, when the sky darkened, stone was still hot to touch, but metal had already gone cold. Night metal cool he called it. Touching the barrel of the cleaned rifle he pondered the difference of rich and poor. He had always been poor. Not as poor as he was now, but poor. He'd owned a small farm in a medium sized village. With his wife, child and storehouse of food behind thick walls of mud he made a life. Until a roaming band conned their way in, looted, raped and destroyed everything. Chris watched his storehouse burn, his wife raped and killed, and his child trampled underfoot. He never found that band, identifiable by the pompous obsession of battle flags to show different clans. If he did however, they would remember him.

Half starved, cold, tired and too dry to cry any more, he'd stumbled upon the bunker and the rest was history. He had little to do with the groups of raiders, but only armed with rocks and wooden staffs they had even less to do with him. Sometimes a village would send a runner, usually a fast teenager, to find him and ask for help, but when they got back there was little to return to. The raiders moved like shadows, in then out without leaving sign of where they went. Chris could track anything in any weathers, his job depended on that. But the raiders were clever and never left sign he could track.

Movement below in the trees caught his eye, bringing him back from the past. A small mammal, maybe a rabbit, bounced along looking for fresh grass. It was thin, ribs through mottled fur, but it still tried. Chris watched it for a while. Fresh meat was always in short supply, and even a half starved rabbit was a good variety. He aimed the rifle, cocked it, then lowered it again. The rabbit, unaware its fate lay in the balance sat still, nibbling grass shoots, making a perfect target. Chris shouldered the rifle and watched until it hopped into the growing darkness before resuming his pacing along the roof.

Three days later they repacked the Land Rover and headed south. Marty had noticed Chris was a bit nervy, as he always was when he sniffed out something. The papers helped, but were too unreliable. One of the things that made Chris so good at his job was the intuitive skill at finding trouble. Though the dinosaurs stank, raiders made mistakes, and the few small predators, like lions, leopards and the increasingly more common wolf packs, tended to leave obvious traces of their passing, it took skill to know where they could be, and where to go to get them. Marty had been riding with Chris for three season cycles and still had no idea how the old man found what he wanted, and usually where he wanted it to be. Sometimes, like the Allosaurus, they just sat waiting to be shot. Others, like a particularly troublesome dog pack, were as chaotic as possible until they got in his sights, then lined up together to die. However he did it Chris did it well. Nothing shocked him, nothing scared him. He just stared down fear and danger until it ran away.

Clean shaven, driving the old Land Rover Chris looked the part. No men shaved in the outside world. Blades were hard to find, old knives usually sharpened to a stub were the best you could find. Chris had cases of razor blades, mountains of soap, and all the luxuries you could want for living outdoors. More than once Marty had suggested selling it. There was a lot to be made from the bunker, and with all the weaponry a small army could take the land and be ruled by Chris as king. Sometimes, in his hammock, Marty would dream of being the prince, fanned by near naked ladies, fed from their clean fingers while below him, others counted his money. Chris had no cares for money, even refusing it when offered for payment. Meat, and a safe corner were his rewards. Marty took what he could.

Their faded and patched camouflaged clothing did certainly help hide from sharp eyes, but mostly it was for comfort. The tough weave shrugged off branches, thorns and stones to save cuts and grazes. Same with the calf high tough boots. Even the seats of the car were from a similar cloth. With a pistol on the hip, pouches on their belts and short, clean hair and chins they looked efficient and prepared. Chris often commented that they were sellers of a service, and had to look right. As best as Marty could tell, that was the only vanity Christopher Spencer had.

"So, where too now then, boss? Got a sniff?" asked Marty, breaking the silence.

Chris nodded. "Something south has been hiding for a while. Think it's the big one that munched that village you liked."

"Yeah," said Marty, "the one with those three fitties?"

"That's the one," said Chris. "It got away from me and I want it. Score to settle. Paper said a convoy had a night hit last week or so. In the dark they lost a tail wagon. No idea why, or where. The next one down saw nothing odd. Guy just drove into the trees."

"Bet he didn't," said Marty.

Chris nodded again. "He didn't. That thing would have nudged him into the woods, then had him before he could shout for help. Get it this time though. Maybe get something from the convoy runners too."

"Doubt it," said Marty. "They'll just say we did it to look like it. You know some don't even believe these things exist?"

"Well, they can't disbelieve when it opens their cabs like a tin can."

"Yeah," said Marty, looking at the stripped Land Rover, with no roof, doors, or windscreen. The rattling machine gun in front of him gave him comfort, and he checked the belt feed to be sure. Chris noticed.

"Don't panic. This is the plains. Nothing here but lost goats, the odd dog, and us."

Marty smiled weakly, then clambered into the back. On the roll cage behind the front seats was the big gun. It fired slugs as thick as his thumb, made a hell of a noise, and went through anything. Marty twisted the clamps free, then spun the whole mount in a 360 degree arc, to check behind. He steadied his hands on the mount as Chris suddenly hit the brakes, hard.

"Wassup?" Marty asked.

"Trouble," Chris replied. He changed from easy relaxed driver to killer instantly. Marty followed suit, clicking the safety catch from the big gun, and scanning the flat grass. Chris had pulled his rifle from the carrier behind his seat, loaded and knelt on the flat bonnet of the car. Nearby, on the still, hot air of midday, the sounds of snoring and grunting carried softly. Chris gave a silent hand gesture, and Marty slid from the big gun, lifting his rifle from the carrier. After a brief look Chris slipped into the knee high grass. Marty waited for a moment, then followed just as silently, a few feet away. They stooped low, keeping as close to the grass as they could. Chris paused, then half raised a hand. Marty froze, and slowly lowered himself to the grass. Before them, in a small hollow in the plain, several men lay sleeping.

They were a band of raiders. Scruffy, with wild hair and beards, they looked like savages. With deep scars from fighting, missing ears and fingers, festooned with sharpened sticks, bones, and even a blade or two, they looked good enough to scare any poor peasant. The shapes of three women, bloody and motionless, lay nearby. They must have had a recent strike. Some food, clothes and even an old earthen jug showed the fruits of their endeavours. Using only eye contact Chris motioned Marty to move back, plucking three grenades from his belt. Marty motioned to the three women, one of whom was just barely moving, barely alive. Chris shook his head, pulled the pins and with a lazy throw, pitched the grenades into the hollow. They dropped to the warm grass, hands over their ears. The grenades exploded with a loud thump that shook the ground around their faces, leaving them coughing. Chris was up in a second and ran into the smoking hollow rifle at his shoulder ready. Marty followed shortly after, trying not to cough. All the raiders were dead. Two of the grenades had seen to that. Marty noticed the third had been thrown amongst to women. He looked questioningly at Chris, who kept his hard stare, then turned and headed back to the car, rifle still raised. Raiders seldom let their whole band sleep at one time. This lot must have been careless.

Back in the car Marty still kept his gaze locked on Chris as he started the diesel engine and carried on.

"What?" Chris asked eventually.

"Those women were still alive," Marty almost pleaded.

"No they weren't. They were dead the moment they got raided. I helped ease their passage to the next world."

Marty sat back. "You don't know that," he said.

"Don't I? Ask yourself how you would feel, knowing your home was gone, your family dead and you raped to death. Would you want to live?"

"You didn't even try to help them."

Chris looked at Marty, who still stared blankly ahead.

"I did. I did the best thing for them. To heal their wounds would leave the scars of the past. And no other village would let them in. They'd die out here, slowly and painfully." Chris still looked at Marty, saw the tear run down his cheek. Without a history everything was new to Marty, and he struggled with difficult situations. If only Marty could remember his past. Looking back to the plains ahead Chris wished he could forget his own.

They found a large village before nightfall. As always they were welcomed warmly. No sensible elder would risk upsetting a Hunter, especially Chris Spencer, the only one with mechanical transport. Marty, as usual, dived into the growing pool of young ladies, his stubbly chin being the cause of much interest. Chris caught up with the locals on all the latest news from the area. As he expected it was fairly quiet. With his efficient skill the deaths and sudden disappearances in the area had dropped steadily. The elder was most interested in the band of raiders they met earlier. They had been threatening the villages, and one nearby was reported by a farmer to be smoking. The elder was glad there were no survivors. After a filling cooked meal of bread, vegetables and some tough cured meat soaked in a soup, Chris unhooked his hammock and slept. Marty joined him later.

As the sun rose so did Chris. He liked sunrise and sunset, but also knew the risks. Animals tended to attack at night, when the dusk fell and most nocturnal creatures were sleepily roaming out. Raiders attacked at dawn, when the first people woke. With his rifle slung Chris climbed the step on the wall all villages had, and paced the mud ledge looking out. Like most villages this one had the huts where they slept, and stored food inside the thick walls, a river nearby, or a well inside the walls, and farms all around. This gave good vision all around, allowing Chris to see a long way out. He saw nothing but the smudge of smoke in the distance, clearly the other village. Winding dirt paths lead from village to village. People didn't travel far if they could avoid it, but they still spoke to neighbours, shared tools and crops, shared advice. The sun was climbing, shortening the shadows. With no breeze it was going to be a hot day again. Chris was about to turn back to the steps down when he paused. There was no breeze yet the grass had been moving. He crept to the ledge and looked again. To the north the grass waved gently, as if an invisible hand were running through the grass. Chris knew what that was. He dropped from the ledge ignoring the steps, and ran to the car. He pushed Marty out of his hammock and dropped his rifle on him. Taking more grenades and magazines Chris headed back to the steps, pausing to hammer on the door of the elders hut.

Once in position Chris quickly checked all around the walls. Only one direction of attack. That meant it was the remainders of the band of raiders. They waving grass followed the twin tracks from their car. As they got closer shapes began to form in the growing light. The raiders had covered themselves in grass to hide. Clever, Chris thought, they nearly had him. Marty slid in beside him. He had his rifle ready, and Chris noticed with satisfaction that even tired Marty had remembered to bring more ammunition and the white grenades that burned rather than exploded. In the grass below the raiders reached the edge of the farmland. There their camouflage wouldn't work, so they stood, and with a blood curdling scream they ran for the main gate. This was open, and with a roar of triumph the raiders ran on, thinking they had caught a big village napping. They were wrong. As the went through the gates three mines laid by Chris exploded. Half were cut down in an instant. The rest, driven by wild screams kept going. The two men on the ledge knelt as fired. Their large calibre rifles split the dawn quiet, throwing round after round into the shrinking band below. What had started as a group of fifteen raiders was now only a couple, who tried to surrender, throwing their weapons away and kneeling down. Marty raised his rifle, showing them he accepted. Chris kept his aim on them. Dropping from the ledge he walked, rifle raised, to the two men.

"How many?" he demanded.

"Just us, just us," the man babbled, tears on his face. His companion, also crying, nodded earnestly. They saw the look in Chris' face and stopped crying. His finger tightened twice and both men lay dead. The villagers watched from behind hut doors. Some ran out to close the heavy wooden gates, kicking motionless bodies out of the way. The elder came last, supported by two men. He laid a hand on Chris' shoulder, smiled his thanks, then was helped back. Watching him go Chris doubted the old man would see another summer.

Marty kept watch on the ledge, just in case, while Chris helped pile the bodies outside. They would be cut up and buried in the farm plots, nutrients for the soil. Chris loaned knives so they could cut up the bodies while he searched their weapons for anything of use. He didn't expect much and found less. Apart from a few old coins from the before time, some trinkets possibly kept as lucky charms, and a strange shaped bone they had nothing of note. Event their clothing, mostly animal skins, was too badly worn to be of use. Anything that couldn't be buried was burned. All day the villagers cleared the evidence of the morning attack while Marty kept constant watch from the ledge. After the sun had reached it's height Chris brought some food in an earthen bowl for him. Marty ate silently.

"Go on, then. Say your piece," Chris said. Marty just munched the stringy vegetable soup. "You know why. Stop giving me the silent treatment."

"You didn't have to kill them," Marty whispered.

"I did, and you know I did. Fear. That's what they use, and that's why we get left alone. Fear, and intimidation. Do you want them running back to their clan leader and telling the tale? You think they'd change and stay here?"

Marty kept his head down over the bowl of soup, as if smelling it. With a barely perceivable movement he shook his head. Chris laid a hand on his shoulder and pulled the young man to his side.

"I don't like it. Killing some remade monster, fine. Random wild animals, ok. But people, and people who made a bad choice? I hate it. I could tie them up, dump them days from here, but if they found their way back." Chris sighed. "I don't want to come back here to find that." He waved a hand vaguely at the distant village.

Marty's head gave a tiny nod.

"Eat your soup, then get some rest. We stay here tonight. Head out after sun up tomorrow."

Chris watched as Marty noisily drained the bowl and dropped off the ledge without a look back. Chris waited until he was out of sight, then reached into his shirt, hand grasping the metal chain that hung there.

One of the men from the village came and sat beside Chris. He touched the stock of his rifle as if it would bite him. He gestured to Chris if he could hold it. Chris shook his head.

"Uh-uh, friend," Chris said, moving the weapon away from the man. "Not safe."

The man looked like crying, then steeled himself.

"You need help? I strong, and smarts. Got mush in here," he said, tapping his skull.

"You do, and have guts too," Chris said. "But I need more than that. And me and Marty have it covered. Thanks, though." Chris rose to walk the wall. Pausing he looked back. The man hadn't moved. "Maybe when we swing back we can chat."

The man smiled a gap toothed smile. "Yar, yar. We chat, we joined up? Me be good helper!" The man leapt down to the beaten earth floor of the village, swaggering like a price winner. Chris watched him go and wondered how far he would get in life. Many tried to rise from the mud, but how? There was nothing to do but farm, eat, reproduce and die. Nothing to rise to. Turning away Chris walked the ledge, then the outside of the wall, checking for weak spots. When Marty relived him that evening Chris made some suggestions to the village elder before returning to his hammock.

Chapter Two

In the biggest city of the country life was as normal. People went to work, they ate, they slept, they woke, they went to work again. Saturday was traders day, where the square outside the government buildings was full of bright coloured stalls, selling food mostly, and samples of equipment. Some recruited for bigger companies, and notice boards advertised the smaller ones. There was no crime here. Doors were unlocked. Simple notices controlled the population. Disobedience meant expulsion from the city, a galling ceremony where the accused were stripped to rags, lead through the streets to the southern gate and sent through while the masses mocked and jeered.

Walking through the thriving market Officer Piers Compton felt useless. He had a good job, a respected job. His glossy bowler hat made him stand out in the bareheaded crowd, his neatly pressed uniform distinguished him from the gauze clad population. Piers didn't feel respected. He felt hot in the merciless sun, sweat soaking his buffed hat, and staining the pure white of his uniform. He was unarmed, weapons were useless in a city of peace, but he carried a belt mounted holster, empty to show honesty of the law enforcement. He had a small torch, that didn't work, and a notepad for notes, but no pencil. He had been an Officer class three for five years, never arrested anyone, never heard of a crime, never saw someone leave by the south gate. Some in the western quarter had some crimes. Mostly these were from convoy drivers unloading or loading. Sometimes the poor area, that was most of the west, had a minor scuffle, but in the richer northern sector where Piers worked it was silent. People nodded a polite greeting as they passed, traders offered food, that he had to refuse, also politely. The whole thing bored Piers. He dreamed of excitement, of adventure. His parents had been well to do. Father was a money man, who dealt with inventory chits and promissory notes. Mother lived at home, naturally. She was a fine woman but like everyone else was muted to the wild outdoors by the massive walls. Sometimes, when off duty, Piers would stand on the north gate and look out. From the high vantage point the could see the glimmer of the ocean on a clear day. Otherwise he was like everyone else, trapped behind the sixty foot high stone walls that surrounded the city, the bastions on the gates were even higher. There were no windows looking out, who would want to?

Roaming without destination, or reason, Piers was supposed to be looking for stall snatchers stealing items, under the counter dealings, and drunks. There was no alcohol in the city, no hidden network of criminals, or anyone risking being caught stealing food and risk being removed from the city. There was a welfare system for the hard up, food for the hungry, even rudimentary healthcare. Everyone was happy in their own little utopia. Everyone except Piers.

Absently walking past the traders he was shocked from his daydream by a scream. The market stopped dead. Nobody screamed any more. This was not a scream of pain, like an accident. This was fear, pure, frozen to the floor fear. Feeling naked without even a staff to fight with Piers ran, aware everyone was looking to him. The scream stopped. Rounding a corner three scared women cried in a huddle, while two men tried to comfort them. All were white as his uniform. One man pointed a trembling finger to the wall opposite. Someone had thrown red paint all over it. Moving closer the smell hit him. The heat of the day making it worse. It wasn't paint. Beside a bent and warped drain lay a foot, the brilliant white of bone sticking out from the red gristle. It was a ladies foot, Piers noticed, the shoe near it was white, but now red with the wearers blood. The drain itself loomed open and black, as if asking him to look inside. Backing away, eyes fixed to the gaping hole, Piers Compton went to report the first incident of his career.

Another sunrise, another village. Chris and Marty had slept rough the night before, being nowhere near anywhere. Neither slept well outside, constant watches were needed to be ready if anything got hungry in the night. This village was prosperous, one of the settlements that had grown over the years, the original low wall still remained, but a taller, stronger outer wall had been made farther out. Newer huts, and even one with a floor above the ground, were spaced openly inside the outer wall. Large food storage huts showed prosperous farming, testimony to the skill of the villagers to use the nearby stream to water their land. There were no threats to them. They had even started on another wall around their farms. Chris wondered if this was how the big cities formed. Marty as usual had dived into the crowd of young ladies around him.

They left early, once the sun was high enough to settle Chris' worry of a morning attack. They were still heading south, nearing one of the less used convoy routes from the big waters to the south. There were no trucks here, and no sign of recent use, the dirt track was slowly being overrun with stubby grass. The area Chris wanted was still a distance away, and Marty worried their fuel wouldn't last.

"We're pretty far off, ain't we?" he asked Chris.

"A bit. We don't go far south much. When did you learn to read the sky?"

Marty shrugged. "Gotta learn sometime," he said.

"Took you long enough." Chris slowed the car. Marty instantly went for his rifle. "Calm yourself, young 'un. Just want to top up."

Marty put his rifle back and searched the area. He couldn't see anything but flat grasslands and the odd stunted tree. Chris pulled up beside a burnt out stump, took his rifle and checked around. Marty climbed into the big guns seat and peddled around in a circle. He knew there was nothing there, but when Chris went hunting he knew there must be something. A low whistle caught his attention and he saw Chris, rifle slung, waving to him.

"Not doing this myself again, kid," he said.

Marty saw he had pulled a wooden cover that was hidden by grass. Below was a rough dug hole in which fuel cans, ammunition and some parts were hidden. Wires trailed the board, a sign of traps set by Chris to stop thieves.

"Whet we taking," Marty asked.

"Just fuel. Got plenty. May need another replen run down here. This is from a couple of years ago, before I found you." Chris heaved a metal fuel can out, closing his eyes from the rust that rained down from it. Marty went for the handle, which broke, and grabbed it by the lip. They worked quickly, aware they made a nice, obvious target. After three large fuel cans they were off again, traps reset before they left.

In the pure white foyer Piers felt immensely scruffy. He hadn't had time to change, or even to wash his sweaty face. And now he was waiting in the thankfully cool reception to the city mayor. Only hours after the 'attack' he had barely filled his report before being summoned.

"Mr Compton? His Lordship will see you now." The immaculate Attendant ushered him, without touching, through the large double doors into the mayors office.

Mayor Alberto Precious sat behind his giant dark wood desk. Neatly stacked on one side were notes, letters and correspondence. On the other was a small metal tube with a cover on to contact the Attendant. The high, wing back chair faced the wide window overlooking the courtyard below.

"Officer Piers Compton, third level sire," the Attendant said, then left.

Silence filled the empty room. Aside from the desk there was no other furnishings. A small door to one side presumably led to another chamber where the mayor could freshen up during the day. It was even colder in here and Piers shivered in his still damp uniform.

Still the silence hung like a cloak, suffocating. Piers felt inclined to speak, but had learned over the years to wait. He had been called, not asked, to see the mayor. When the mayor was ready he would speak. Feeling like he was being tested Piers stood firmly to attention and waited. Finally the cream chair turned.

Mayor Precious was a large man, his extra chin hung low enough to half hide the white neck tie he wore. His shirt was also white, but billowed like soft cotton. Short haired, going thin Piers noted, and clean shaven he looked the prosperous ruler of a prosperous city. And he had to be. The richest became mayor, the theory being anyone who made the most notes was the best organiser. A heavy brow hooded clever dark eyes.

"So, Compton?" he spoke with a deep, booming voice.

"Sire!" Piers tried to stand even more to attention.

"I have your report here, Compton. Sounds a little strange to me." Precious waved a sheet of paper vaguely before neatly dropping it back on the centre of the desk. "Five witnesses, all conflicting statements. Sure you got it right?"

"They all spoke under oath, sire," Piers replied. The big man with the big voice was intimidating, making him feel small.

Precious paused while he openly looked Piers over. He did not seem impressed with the slender young man with the dirty uniform.

"I feel this would be best handled by a higher level officer. I have passed it through to Internal Investigations. They will handle it. I trust you will give them all the help you can?"

"Of course, sire," Piers replied, knowing it wasn't really a question.

"Very well. And please try to maintain your appearance. You are supposed to set an example. Your record is sketchy at the very best. If you wish to obtain that fourth bar you have some way to go."

Piers nodded. "Yes, sire."

"Dismissed, Officer," the mayor said, waving him away. He opened the flap of his speaking tube and spoke softly. Piers paused for a moment, raised his left arm out straight in salute, turned smartly and left.

Outside the Attendant had his ear to the tube, and offered the trace of a sympathetic nod to Piers as he left. Climbing the long stairs down to the courtyard Piers felt a failure again. The first real piece of action and he was taken off it. He knew I.I. were the ones to deal with this, but as the first on the scene Piers felt responsible. Not that I.I. would even speak to him. They had names and locations of the witnesses, all his statements and initial report. He would probably only be mentioned in the paper as 'an officer of the law'. His time of duty over Piers wandered the clean streets thinking. Pausing on Main Bridge he watched the river lazily trickle below. The hot weather had dried the bed into crazy blocks of mud. Drifting more he found himself outside one of the less impressive bars near the west gate. He had been here before as a child, chatting to convoy drivers. Feeling the need for excitement he glanced around, then slid in through the half door.

Inside the warmth still hung in the air, but the light did not. A long bar took up half the room on three side. Young ladies in a weird uniform served unkempt men their cold drinks, non alcoholic, and the smell of burnt food wafted from the kitchen out back. Dropping into an empty table away from the door Piers waited. Finally a tired waitress asked his order and headed back through the muted conversations. Clearly a convoy had just arrived, the drivers and crew relaxing after a risky trip. Piers moved a little closer to the main group to hear what they said.

"Tellin' ya, them stories are true," one man mumbled.

"Rubbish!" retorted another. "Monsters I ask you. Just an excuse. Those who fall behind do it because they found some glug. Drunkards the lot."

"I seen one," said the first. "Tall it were, like a tree, but had two legs, a big long tail, and teeth that went on forever."

"Teeth? You mean like these?" the second man asked, removing a half set of dentures from his mouth.

"They go forever," said a third.

The group laughed.

"What about the nutter we saw on the way here?" asked another. The small man looked new and was openly scorned by the veterans.

"'im? 'e were nuthin' but trash. Driftin' about like weeds waiting to find some poor fool to cheat. Bet he made up them tales of yours," said the second, nudging the first man.

"You know who that were? That Hunter bloke. Only guy here with wheels," the first man said, a little louder. "He's the one who get 'em."

"Hunter!" the second man said. "Only thing 'e 'unts is notes and nookie."

"He does," said the newcomer. "Heard from another convoy. He finds the things, or raiders, or whatever, and gets them. Never misses. Spencer, his name is."

"Conman, 'is name is," said the second. "Don't care much 'bout 'im. Don't wanna hear more." He finished his drink and stood, the others followed. "Come on you lot. Need to prep them trucks or we'll miss the times." He walked pass the bar, dropping a note to the girl, and left. Piers waited a moment, then followed.

He trailed them to the drivers area, where they slept when not on the road. As they got close the newcomer held back, reading a notice. The others left him. Seeing his chance Piers stood beside him.

"Hello," Piers said, pretending read the note.

"Hey, sir," replied the newcomer nervously. An officer here was rare, a level three was rarer. Already he looked for an escape route, just in case.

"Relax. I'm not on time. Just wandering the city

looking around. I work the north side. I heard your chat in the bar. Who is Spencer?"

The newcomer dropped his shoulders and leant on the notice. "Some drifter. Seems to find everything he needs out there. No idea how, mind."

Piers nodded. "Where did you meet him?"

The man looked upwards thinking. "On the west road, about three or four days ago. Don't know where he was headed, or why. Won't be there now. His kind don't stop, just drift."

"How did you know it was him? Surely there must be others around?" Piers took a small pad from his hip and penned some notes with a pencil he had taken from his desk.

"Easy. Only one with wheels. There are a few, mostly with spears and blades. This guy had a half truck, guns and some sort of uniform. Rides with a younger guy too. Always together. Only seen them once, but all the drivers know of him."

"Thank you," said Piers, taking notes. "And you said about this monster?"

"Ah, yar. There's raiders, animals, and hairless monsters that eat you whole. Loads of them out there, less animals now. Mostly eat the scummy villages. Not seen one," he leant closer and spoke softly, "but sometime a truck leaves the convoy and is never seen again. Sometimes they just stop. Always in the dark, never a sound. Just vanish."

Piers found himself drawn into the image of a huge dog like creature, hairless and fierce, eating the huge trucks whole. Coming back to reality the man had gone, pleased with the break to slip away. The image of the dog thing still in his head Piers wondered if there was a link, and if so, what could he do.

Chapter Three

The east and south of the city was laid out with storehouses, factories, offices and a small dock on the shrunken river. The rich travelled north in their man powered carts, the poorer walked west over the Lesser Bridge to their condensed rooms. One man had finished his time of work and headed out with the rest of the crowd. Some used the tunnels under the ground, left from the before time, to escape the sun. The man decided not to this time. As he passed the steps to the tunnels people began running out. Pushed by the tide of terrified bodies the man tried to hold onto a low wall, but was swept along. Looking back he saw someone run from the dark entrance, only to be pulled back by a small, hairless shape with large teeth. The man stopped struggling and ran.

Piers was also passing a tunnel entrance when panicked people streamed out. Pressing himself against some railing he managed to keep his position. As the flood thinned he heard a whimpering inside the tunnel. Cautiously he crept into the darkness. Discarded papers, food boxes, even clothes were strewn on the floor. As his eyes grew accustomed to the dark Piers saw the shape of a body on the ground. As he got closer it moved. He was about to go and help them when he saw a snake rise up, moving around slowly. The snake turned, and he saw the outline clearly of a two legged creature, almost as tall as a man, with a long tail behind, short arms, long neck leading to a boxy head. The head split in two as the jaws opened. Blood glistened dark on white teeth like knives. The head sniffed the air, then snapped towards him. The creature turned and hissed like a dying man. Piers forgot about his duty, turned, and ran for his life. He didn't stop until he was far from the tunnel, his heart pounding through his chest, lungs on fire. Only when his body gave out did he stop, sink to the floor and gasp.

Chris found the village he wanted, but no sign of the thing he was after. It had moved away was all the locals could say. Annoyed at the time wasted he headed back north. He wanted to pass the big city and go back to his bunker. It was time for a break. Collect all the meat he had stored and relax before the weather turned. It was nearing the wet season. Clouds, dark and menacing, were forming on the horizon, a sign the cold winds and snow would be coming soon. The cycle was nearly over and they needed to change hot clothes for cold. He had no intention of being caught out in the cold. Word from some villagers spoke of trouble in the big city. Chris didn't care, and ignored them. Marty searched every bit of information he could. As far as Chris was concerned the cities were due some trouble. As long as it was there he had less to worry about here. They thanked the elder for his kindness and headed north.

Piers once again sat outside Mayor Precious' office. This time he was cleaned and smart. Boots buffed, bowler hat brushed clean, shirt pressed. The Attendant gave another apologetic look as if to say: sorry you are here twice in one day. Again he was ushered in, still not touched.

"Officer Compton, sire."

Mayor Precious was flanked by two men this time, all looking at a map of the city on his desk. One wore the white shirt and bowler of an officer of the law, with five bars and a star; chief of the law. The other wore black, black shirt, black pantaloons, black boots. An Internal Investigations agent. Piers felt the damp sweat of fear form on his brow. This man could have him removed for no reason at all. Awesome was their power. The mayor looked up from the map.

"Ah, Compton. Finally. You didn't need to get changed. we needed your report as soon as possible. Lives are at risk and you swan off to get cleaned up."

"Sorry, sire." Piers tried to avoid the man in blacks gaze.

"Well, you're here now," said Precious. "Report, man. And be quick about it."

Piers told in as much detail as he could what had happened. He included every detail of the tunnel, it's location, position of the sun and the creature he saw. He omitted his trip to the drivers bar, or his conversation with the man there. When he finished the chief of the law glared at him as if he felt his own kind had failed him. The I.I. agent put a small black notepad back into his pocket and lessened his gaze. Mayor Precious remained irritated.

"So you ran then?" he asked with distain.

"I saw little I could do unarmed against such a threat, sire, so retreated to give a report instead." Piers bristled slightly under the accusation of cowardice. He was not much in the grand scheme of things, but he was no coward.

"You ran. Clearly not officer material?" the mayor asked, turning to the chief of the law, who still stared at Piers like he was a criminal.

"Clearly," the chief rumbled.

"May I speak, sire?" asked the agent. His squeaky voice was almost comical, but Piers knew not to laugh.

"If you wish, Agent Parks," said Precious, as if he didn't really care. He looked back to the map. The chief kept his withering stare.

"Officer Compton, you said this thing was consuming a body?"

"Yes, Agent Parks," Piers replied as confidently as he could. The air felt colder now.

"And this creature was slightly shorter than a man, but was," he paused to retrieve his notes, "kneeling down. Is this correct?"

"Yes, Agent Parks."

"Thank you, Officer Compton. I'm sure you have duties to return to, does he Chief of the Law?"

"He does," rumbled the chief with great disgust.

"Dismissed," said Precious without looking from his map.

Piers felt he had been let off a very nasty hook, tried hard not to smile and left.

As he walked back to his post Piers heard steps trying to catch up with him. Turning he saw Agent Parks, now in his uniform robe, striding to join him. Resisting the urge to run he waited for the dark man.

"Thank you, Officer Compton. As I grow older my mobility wanes." Parks looked only slightly older the Piers, but the toll of high office must have taken something off the man.

"Any time, Agent Parks," replied Piers.

"I wished to speak with you away from your superiors as one item of your report puzzles me. Why were you on the west side?"

"I merely wished to stretch my legs after the shock of this mornings find, Agent Parks," said Piers.

"Ah, stretch your legs. Did you stretch them to any particular destination?"

"No, Agent Parks. I did pass a drivers bar, just to check for disturbances. One had recently arrived."

"True," said Parks. "Did this recent convoy have any interesting tales?"

Piers thought for a moment. What harm could it do?

"I did find one thing of note. These incidents happen in the outside as well, Agent Parks."

"And was there no other information?" Parks had resumed his note taking.

"Just there was a reliable man to remove these threats. Spencer, or Spender I think his name was."

Parks nodded. "Christopher Spencer. We are aware of him. Did you happen upon a description of him?"

"I only heard he travels with a companion, and is the only one with transport."

"This we knew, Officer Compton. Do you feel you could identify him?"

Piers shrugged. "Possibly, Agent Parks, but not in here."

Parks reached inside his robe and withdrew a folded piece of paper. Handing it to Piers he nodded and left.

Alone Piers opened the roll. On it was a permit to travel, used only for drivers and outcasts. This was for Piers to leave with the next convoy. Inside was a smaller note. Hand written it said briefly: find Spencer and bring him to me. Don't return alone. Agent Parks., I.I. Folding the paper up Piers shuddered. He had never left the city. Nobody did. He dreamed of it, only because it would never happen. Now he was being told to. Outside. Where people were wild, were killed, had 'accidents'.He was being sent into the wilderness to find a man who hard to find. And to bring him back? What with? He had no authority to promise anything. But when an agent tells you to do something you were wise not to ask questions. Piers opened the roll again. Departure was the next morning. Just enough time to pack.

As the dawn broke, the cool of the night already passing like a fond memory, Piers Compton knocked on the dispatch office near the west gate. He still wore his uniform, and carried a weave pack with a spare uniform and boots. The note hadn't said what he was supposed to do about joining a convoy, or what excuse he was to give. After a sleepless night in his quarters he decided to claim to be a legal envoy, complete with a roll of orders to the convoys stops, delivering updates on changes to laws. This was plausible as with his low level he would be likely to be dropped with such a duty. After a brief explanation to an uninterested attendant he was directed through to the staging area.

He found himself in a large open area, the sky already a deep blue overhead. The noise of shouting men, clanking machinery and banging from mechanics deafened him. In the centre of the staging area, facing the gate leading to the west gate, lay twelve trucks, lined side by side. They were loaded from a ramp at the back.

The crates each with only an identification number burned on were pushed on with squealing trolleys. Men shouted for different crates, while others with rolls marked off what was on which truck. At the front mechanics were refitting the metal shields to the cabs, while checking the engines worked. Black smoke hung in the air like fog. A quick search led Piers to the drivers shed where they checked their packs, drew whatever they felt they needed, and had a last drink before leaving. The newcomer was there, and quickly looked away as Piers stepped in. the door closed behind by itself, shutting out the din. It felt too quiet to Piers, until he realised everyone was watching him silently. An officer of the law didn't wander into drivers sheds.

Nervously he raised a hand. "Greetings. I have been ordered to accompany this trip. Got updates to deliver." he patted his weave pack. Slowly the conversations resumed. Piers sat at an empty table. The big man from the bar stood and came over.

"What does an officer of the law want?" he asked.

"Merely to travel somewhere. I need no special treatment, just passage."

"We ain't no tour coach, sir," the man managed to make 'sir' sound rude. "We only have space for men who work."

"What can I do to help?"

The man laughed. "What can you do?"

"I have many skills as an officer of the law." Piers stood and faced the drivers. "My name is Officer Piers Compton, level three. I have be instructed to deliver updates. If anyone does not wish to help me they can certainly take it up with my superiors who will be very interested to hear as to why."

The man grunted and left. Another came over.

"Tom Greer. I drive 22. Got no lookout so you can ride with me. Ever driven a long truck?"

Piers looked around, feeling he was under some sort of test, and on the edge of winning and losing.

"Never even driven a short truck, Mr Greer."

The room erupted in laughter and jeers. The drivers stood, some even clapping him roughly on the back. Feeling accepted it was clear to Piers that he had passed.

"Come with me, officer. Let's get you settled in the Double Duck," Tom said, and led the way. Piers was now an honorary driver.

Chapter Four

Double Duck, or number 22, was the same as the other trucks, with only a stencilled number on the front and sides to separate it. Beside the numbers on the articulated cab was a hand drawn logo of two yellow ducks, with a white back in the shape of a number two on each. Climbing the retractable ladder Tom showed Piers the interior. The armour plates blocked most of the light, but the dim beam from the roof hatch showed a small bed at the back, two seats in the front, and little else.

"Sleep there," Tom pointed first to the bed, "eat there," then the front seat without a wheel, "crap over the side. Food is in the hatch in the back. You sit here most of the day," he gestured to a fold down seat inside the hatch allowing him to sit half outside the cab. "No far seers so just have to use your eyes. See anything shout it down. Don't fall off, don't fall asleep and don't fart. Understand?"

"Sounds fairly simple. What do we do?" Piers slung his weave bag onto the bed.

"We do nothing. I drive, you look. Stops on the route are only at night at safe places. We don't stop before or after. Truck breaks down the one behind pushes them. We don't get people who fall off." Tom dropped into the drivers seat and started flipping switches. Piers sat beside him.

"So I just look around?" Piers asked.

"Basically. Normally we change but I doubt you have ever driven."

"Not really. Tried out once for mobile patrol, but didn't get in."

Tom stopped his preparations and gave Piers a long searching look. He turned the key and the Double Duck shook violently before the engine caught and settled into a gentle vibration. They were third from last, and they waited for the others to leave before slotting in behind number 74. Dust already started blowing around the windowless cab, making Piers cough. Tom handed him a spare dust mask, then fitted his own. With goggles and head scarf Piers thought he looked quiet frightening and began to enjoy the trip. Tom sang songs remarkably well, although they weren't songs the Compton family would like. Songs of loose women, easy money, and the benefits of both. Tom waved him up to the hatch. The seat wasn't that bad, and with his feet up above the seats Piers found he could get reasonably comfortable. The breeze kept the heat off, and the head scarf stopped the suns glare in his eyes.

The line of smoke belching trucks headed away from the sun, chasing their shadows. As the sun rose higher Tom tapped Piers's leg, calling him down. He offered a tin mug of warm water.

"So what's the real reason?" Tom asked.

"Real reason?" said Piers.

"For being out here. Updates are sent the same as everything else, in the back. So why you here? Running?"

Piers shook his head. "Sent by I.I. Special task. This is a cover."

Tom looked impressed, thinking Piers to be some undercover agent.

"You go all the way then, Agent?"

"As far as I need to," said Piers. "And don't call me Agent."

"Of course. What do I call you, Agent?"

Piers thought as he watched the plains pass by. The city, his home, had long since vanished in the haze. All alone out here he felt very vulnerable. But also accepted more than he had been before.

"Call me Piers. Or Officer when the others are listening."

"Ok, Piers," said Tom.

Piers finished the cup and went back up top. He looked out hard as any other, but he was looking for something they weren't. He was looking for a solitary car in a massive plain of nothing.

Half a day away Chris and Marty were having troubles. One of the big problems with using ancient equipment was it failing. Two of the Land Rovers tyres had decided to give up on a particularly rough bit of the plain. Changing them was proving hard. The ground was soft so the jack they had just sank. In the end Chris was forced to creep forwards following Marty until they found harder ground. Both knew if they were surprised they would be forced to leave the car, detonating the ammunition, and flee on foot. Chris scanned the horizon while Marty scuffed his boots in the arid soil until he finally found a plank of wood they could use under the jack. They had lost half a day to the flats and were unlikely to find a village before dark. As they changed the wheels Marty noticed a smudge on the hazy plain. Chris inwardly cursed his failing eyesight and dropped the tools. Pulling his rifle and far seers he inspected the smudge.

"Convoy. Coming from the big city by the looks of it. No threat." He dropped from the flat bonnet of the car and slid the rifle into its carrier. "Need this done fast though."

"Getting another paper?" Marty asked, taking the far seers from Chris.

"Maybe. You wanting the latest city news?"

"Sure," said Marty, his back to Chris. "See if anything interesting has happened."

Chris grunted with a stiff nut. "In the city? Nothing interesting happens. Their life is: 'I got up, ate, went to work, came home, ate, went to sleep'. boring."

Marty smiled as he watched the convoy. "Not like here," he said.

"Nope," replied Chris. "Imagine them out here?" Chris stood and clapped his hands on his face in mock shock. "Oh no, the tyre is flat. whatever shall I do? Oh, help me please, somebody!" He danced around shouting for help while Marty creased up in laughter. Eventually Chris dropped the charade and changed the wheel. "That's what you do. See a problem, fix it, move on. Easy. Now one more to do."

They had the wheels changed soon and decided to meet the convoy and ask for a paper. Marty was excited, leaning forwards as if to try and speed the car on. Chris leant back in his usual relaxed pose.

On the Double Duck Piers strained to see anything in the heat haze. Anything over a few hundred feet faded to a blur. Chatter over the trucks radio made him duck his head inside the cab.

"Understood," said Tom to the hand held microphone. "Check around up there, Piers. Got some trouble ahead. Maybe a raider scout."

Piers sat up and wished for a weapon. Straining to see through the dust lifted by the trucks in front he tried to see anything. Then Tom called him back down.

"Don't panic. Just some drifter. They said he's in some sort of trailer thing. Must be fun pulling that by hand in this heat. Maybe some travelling salesman. Well, we ain't stopping for him."

Disappointed Piers went back up top. He looked out for the sellers trailer but couldn't see far ahead. A deep drone seemed to be getting closer. He tried to place it, but couldn't. With the noise of the truck, the wind and banging from the trailer behind them it was hard to find anything.

"Hail, driver!"

The voice scared the life from Piers. Looking wildly around he saw a man peering over the edge of the cab. The young man, dressed in some sort of camouflage clothing smiled cheerfully.

"Hail, driver. Any news?"

Leaning over the cab Piers saw a four wheeled car, with guns, two people, and loads of attitude. The drone was the cars engine.

"Beat it, freaks!" yelled Tom.

"Aw, I just want the latest roll, driver," called back the young man.

"Leave it, Marty," said another voice. "They won't help you this time. No papers in this thick lot."

"They must have one," replied the young man, precariously hanging on to a large gun mounted on the back of their car.

"You Spencer?" called Piers.

"He is, I'm not," answered the young man. "Why?"

"I have a job for you. Stay there!" Piers dropped back into the cab. "Sorry, Tom. Duty calls you know. Thanks for it all." he grabbed his weave bag and climbed onto the roof. Tom caught his foot.

"Go easy, Agent. Good luck." They shook hands, then Piers dropped his bag to the young man. The ground sped below faster than Piers thought possible. The other trucks sounded their horns, deafeningly. Knowing it could go badly wrong Piers took a deep breath and dropped. The young man caught him and turned so they both fell onto the load bed of the car, taking the inertia from Piers's drop. The driver slowed and turned from the convoy so to clear the dust cloud, stopping a few hundred feet from the trail. Piers stood on the back of the car and faced the two men.

One was young, slender and very healthy looking. The other taller, just, and more stocky, but not fat. Both were tanned, toned and every bit like their descriptions.

"Hello." Piers held out a hand, hanging there as neither men moved. "Piers Compton, officer level three."

Still neither moved. "I've been sent to find you. The mayor needs your help."

"My help?" the stocky man asked.

"Yes, sir. We, um, have a problem." Piers lost all his confidence from the drivers, withering under their eyes. The chief and Parks were powerful, but that was given authority. These men were a different kind of power, one that would leave you dead.

"What kind of problem?" said the stocky man.

"One only Christopher Spencer can help with," said Piers.

"One only Christopher Spencer can help with," the

man repeated. "Hear that, Marty? Only Christopher Spencer can help them. And you just jumped from a moving truck to me. So how you getting home, Officer?"

"Um," Piers squirmed a little as what he had done dawned upon him.

"I think this man needs our help more than his mayor, eh, Marty?"

Marty nodded. The stocky man smiled, softening his hard face instantly.

"Best be getting in the back then, Officer. You have some explaining to do, but not here. Too open. Need to find shelter first."

Chris got in the drivers seat and fired the engine. Marty sat beside him, leaving Piers to sit as best he could in the back.

The nearest village was a miserable sprawl of crumbling huts and half a wall. Parking inside the dilapidated shelter Chris began questioning Piers. Marty unusually left the female population alone to sit in. Over boiled vegetable soup they passed the tin around and talked.

"So, Officer, why you out here looking for us?" Chris asked, never moving his gaze from the dishevelled Piers.

"I have been sent direct from the mayors office to find you. We have an outbreak of something. It's killing people all over the city. We need someone to find it."

Chris took a swig from the dented tin pan and passed it to Marty. "So you need us?"

"Yes," said Piers. "We have no way to deal with this. We have no crime, no defence forces, no soldiers. I don't even get sent out with a pencil, let alone a gun. We don't have the resources to deal with this. We need someone who does."

"Why should I help you, and your mayor?" Chris asked. Marty slurped loudly from the tin, and passed it back to Chris.

"He is willing to pay you for your work," said Piers, knowing he had no authority.

"How much?"

"I don't know." Piers dropped his shoulders, and is act. "To be fair I was told to come and find you. I don't know what's in it for you, or any real reason to come. But I do know I can't go back alone."

Chris drank deeply, then passed the tin to Piers. "Eating people? You get any description without your pencil?"

"Yes," said Piers. "Almost as tall as a man, long head,

loads of teeth, long tail. Saw it myself."

Chris leant forward, eyes burning with the reflection of the fire they sat around, his attention suddenly serious.

"Colour?" he asked.

"It was dark," admitted Piers. "And I was scared. It may have been a green, or brown. All I know is when it looked at me I just ran."

"Lucky you," said Chris, leaning back. "You have a nasty little visitor. And they never travel alone, so you must have a pack there. Minimum four or five. Only ever faced one pack before, in the open, in ground I knew. Your city is as unfamiliar to me as it is to them. But they have the advantage; they were there first, and they know where they are. To go in there after them, on their own ground, would be suicide. Sorry, Officer, but I can't help you."

Piers looked ready to cry. "But you are the best. Everyone knows of you. You are the only one who could stop them."

"I am the best," Chris admitted. "But I am the best because I know when to walk away. Dying to help your reputation isn't much of a bonus. I hunt, I eat, I move on. In your city I'll have people in the way, buildings, your tunnels. All kind of obstructions. I won't be welcomed with open arms, won't be helped. Out here I help by just being here. People welcome me because they know they are safe while I am here. In your city they will just see outsiders. People to mock and scorn. Not really a good reason to go."

"But if you do your job you will be welcomed," said Piers.

"No I won't. I'll still be scorned. Sorry but I prefer to live and help people, not be a thing to be used until it's purpose is done." Chris took back the untouched tin from Piers, drained it and stood.

"There is nothing in there for me. Your people keep people like me out. You deal with it." Chris started to walk back to the car.

Marty stood and ran to catch Chris. Piers just stared into the dying fire.

"C'mon, boss. We can do this," said Marty.

"No we can't," said Chris, still walking. Marty caught his elbow and turned him around.

"We have to. We don't choose the bigger villages because we get more food, we go where we are needed." Marty shook his head. "We are needed there."

Chris looked into his eyes. Marty knew that look and it frightened him. It wasn't anger, or confrontation. It was fear.

"You don't understand, Marty. What they have is bigger than us both. One dino we can deal with, a small pack on the plains we can track. In that stone forest we can't. none of our skills will help. And it's no ordinary animal this time. This is much worse."

"What is it?" asked Marty.

"Bloody Deinonychus, that's what. Juvenile by the sounds of it. Never stop, never tire. Tough to kill, usually finds you first and by then it's too late."

"Sounds like you faced some before," said Marty.

Chris turned and stood looking across the plains. The dusk had settled, bright stars emerging overhead. Silence but the muted conversation from the villagers, crackle of their fire, and insects singing. After a long pause Chris spoke. This was a new Chris, one quiet, timid and almost scared.

"I did once. Many years ago. Had a guy like you rolling with me. We found their nest easily enough. Set charges, was already to leave, blow the nest and go. Then we found they never left. They watched us so silently even I didn't realise they were there. They got him first. Not even time to draw his pistol. I had mine when they pounced. I was lucky. Moved just as they attacked. Clipped one, then another. Got my rifle and put round after round into them. All six died, eventually. Even if you shot a foot away, or a aimed hit to the face they kept coming. Never saw anything like it. Never want to again."

Marty realised Chris was crying, something he had never saw before, and it worried him even more. Chris was always a great source of strength to him. No matter what happened he just shrugged it off and carried on.

"Boss, it's not easy, but we gotta look. Just look," Marty said.

Chris raised his head and cuffed his cheeks dry. Red rimmed eyes turned to face the firelight.

"Just look, and we do it our way," he said eventually. Marty nodded.

They rejoined Piers by the fire who looked almost pleadingly at them.

"We go in we do it our way. Everyone leaves us alone, gets out the way. First sign of oppression we leave," Chris said in his normal tone.

"Agreed," Piers said with tears of relief in his eyes. Marty suppressed a shudder.

"We go at first light. Get some sleep." Chris drew his rifle from the carrier, and walked away. Marty smiled at Piers and set up his hammock. A bit lost Piers looked for a place to sleep, then curled up on the dirt floor near the fire.

Chapter Five

The following afternoon they drew near to the city walls. Chris had never been so close before. What appeared like dull grey walls of smooth stone looked patchy and multicoloured up close, showing repairs and improvements. There were no windows anywhere, but there were small ledges with covered doorways which allowed lookouts to watch and speak. From several of these figures watched the battered Land Rover as it rolled along the beaten dirt track to the West Gate. Before them, jutting from the wall, was a large extension of stone, with more lookout nooks. On the sides ladders were stored, ready to be dropped if needed. Under a stone hood in the centre were the arched twin doors, both thick wood. Above the arch more lookouts stood, holding what looked like bows. The whole design spoke of one thing: security. Anyone trying to fight their way in would be killed before they got close. This had no outside affect on Chris. He drove up to the doors until a voice ordered him to stop.

"Greetings, city dwellers," he called. "We have been sent for by your mayor."

"Of course you have. I'm afraid he's busy now. Maybe come back another day, or never," the lookout called back.

"Ok," said Chris, throwing the car in reverse. Piers jumped out before it moved.

"Hail, observer. I am Officer of the Law Piers Compton as sent by Internal Investigations. I demand you grant us passage."

"Internal, you say," called the lookout. "You're external, Officer. I don't deal with external affairs."

Piers suppressed a curse. "Open up, or you can explain to Agent Parks why you turned the city's salvation away."

"Salvation!" Laughter rolled around the manned posts. "They look like they couldn't save a lost goat."

Chris bridled. He wasn't used to being mocked, not by those who lived long. He stood from his seat, still in the car, and raised his pistol. Thumbing the safety he fired into the air. The echoing shot silenced the laughter.

"I am Christopher Spencer. I am a Hunter. I have been asked by your mayor to come and discuss a matter of security. If you want to stop us, good luck. Now open the gate before I open it for you." He sat, engaged first gear, and pulled forward. The lookout hesitated, then called down to open the outer gate. He also sent a runner into the city. Once they were in the waiting area it wasn't his problem.

The car rolled into the space between the outer and inner gate. Here the walls were ringed with a fire step bristling with arrows and clubs. Chris wasn't surprised they needed him armed as they were. Even their white tunics gave no impression of power, and Chris knew white showed blood better. Bad for inexperienced guards. The outer door banged shut, operated by levers above them. The inner door stayed closed. In the confined space Chris shut off the engine. He still had his pistol in hand, Marty on the big gun, Piers in the passenger seat. After what seemed like hours the inner door creaked open, letting light, and heat, flood in. without a word Chris started the diesel engine and drove through.

Once in the city Chris was instantly lost. The roads were stone, worn smooth. Raised walkways of stone lined the roads. The traffic was light, only carts pulled by sweating young men, delivering goods. The houses loomed high on all sides. This was not safe and Chris whistled gently. Piers almost missed it, but the click from the big gun made him realise it was a code; be ready. Chris laid the pistol on his lap and tried to work out where to go. His vision was blocked by tall buildings to only a few feet. There were no signs, but a large gated yard ahead seemed busy. A convoy staging area he guessed. This was laid out like no village he'd ever stayed in. Unsure what to do he was saved by the appearance of a buggy driven by a smartly dressed man.

It hummed like electric, seated six under an open canopy, but only had four in. Three of them were armed with cross bows.

The buggy stopped in front of them. The driver stayed, but the three armed men jumped off and surrounded the car. Marty swung the gun to face the buggy, Chris instinctively drawing the pistol from his lap, aimed at the nearest man. Piers, however, was already running to stop them. He spoke briefly to one of them, too quiet for Chris to hear, then they both walked back.

"This is Senior Officer of the Law Henderson," said Piers. "He insists you cannot drive through the city armed. You can leave the car here and they will drive you to the mayor."

"No chance," said Chris. "This is a complete deal. Either the car comes with, or we all go our separate ways."

Henderson tried to look tough, but failed under Chris' glare. Eventually he waved a hand. The men climbed back on the buggy, which turned around and waited.

"Guess we follow," said Piers.

Another buggy of armed guards slotted in behind as they were led through the streets. The start of the trip was through high, close cliffs of shaped stone, plain and unimpressive. People in gauzy white cloth, stained and tattered roamed the clean walkways. As they headed north the houses became smaller, and more ornate. The clothing also became cleaner, brighter with colours cropping up. Chris tried to avoid looking at Marty. Most of the best dressed village girls wore animal skins cut suggestively. These ladies wore gauze and little else. It also seemed the larger the cloth, the more important the person. Some walked wearing hardly anything, while others were nearly smothered. After a while Chris realised it wasn't a status symbol, but just price and age. The older wore more as they had more money.

They crossed a nearly dry river by a long, level stone bridge. Large stone cats with plumes of hair on their necks stood guard on each end, and at the centre. Crossing the bridge the road led them through ornate houses, most with grass green and lush outside. Some were three levels even. Walls and gates circled them. The sign of wealth sickened Chris, who knew the hardships of the outside. It seemed some lived in their own little village, just one family where five could live.

Winding through the large houses Piers didn't look. He knew this area well, his parents owned one of these houses. Before it was a sign of comfort, of aspiration. His area of duty wasn't far from here. Now, having spoken to Tom the driver, seen villagers living from clay pots in mud huts this all seemed showy, like boasting. Suddenly home didn't feel like home.

Ahead was a lower wall to the main outer wall. This was maybe twenty feet tall, with no lookout ledges, but there was a gate. Unlike the outer wall gates these were made of bars so you could see inside. It looked metal, but hard to tell. Some sort of crest was laid into each gates bars, looking like the cats from the bridge. In front of the gates two guards with unloaded crossbows stood in small stone huts big enough for one man only. They didn't move as the gates creaked open. Without slowing the buggy drove into the courtyard and stopped.

Marty watched Chris with more than a little apprehension as they sat in the gleaming white reception waiting for the mayor. He looked more irritable than ever. Piers didn't know his little moods, how he hid his feelings, but could be boiling inside. Right now Chris looked ready to snap, sat in brooding silence. Marty himself was excited, and scared. He had never met a high up official before, and tried to work out if it could mean something big for their future. Maybe one of the large, fancy homes with its own wall and even green grass. Piers was also excited and scared. For him this could mean promotion, favours and an easier life, or it could mean removal to the outcasts gate. Chris didn't think of anything other than the cool breeze of the plains, far below, that he missed deeper then he wanted to accept.

The Attendant came over and bowed stiffly. "The Mayor will see you now," he said with dull, practised courtesy. He opened the double doors to the mayors office, and bowed to the unseen desk. "Christopher Spencer, Martin Fritz Herbert, and Officer of the Law Piers Compton, sire," he crooned. A grunt from inside gave vague acceptance. Marty stood and followed the gesture of the Attendant. Piers quickly followed, then paused. Chris still sat. With a low moan he stood and walked into the office.

"His Greatness, Mayor Precious of Laden," announced the Attendant. Piers took a step to one side, Marty off centre, so Chris stood directly in front of the mayor, and struggled not to laugh. Piers looked pained, and Marty surprised, but Chris was going red, tears welling as he choked the giggles inside. Mayor Precious was the largest man he had ever seen, looking like a bird swallowing an egg whole, prettied up in fancy white cloth below a red face he looked ridiculous. He reminded Chris of a man from his childhood. He used to paint his face red from the soil where they butchered meat, and cavort around singing badly and making everyone laugh.

Precious didn't look impressed, going two shades darker. He waited for Chris to control himself and tried not to look too unwelcomingly at him. He saw a stocky, tatty man like a beggar, his clothes different shades of green, brown and black like an accident on an artists palate. He also noticed with anger the men were still armed, both with a metal gun on their hips.

"So you are the great Hunter?" asked Precious with open scorn.

"And you are the 'great' mayor?" replied Chris.

Precious shot Piers a scalding glance then took a pad of paper for notes.

"Do you know what to do, great Hunter?"

Chris visibly bridled, then spoke through gritted teeth. "Yes."

"Do you know what we have here?" Precious kept his head down over the pad.

"You have fat people, with fat pockets and fat rulers," said Chris. Precious looked up, ready to retaliate, but paused. There had been three more attacks since Piers had been sent by that interfering Parks. The people were nervous, and his position was at risk. He needed this man, and his metal gun. Didn't mean he had to like it.

"I feel we got off to a bad start," he said, placing the pad down and leaning back. "You need something, I'm sure. We need this problem gone. We can trade."

Without permission Chris sat on the only other chair in the room, a large armchair in the corner reserved for

Precious to look out the courtyard with ease. Seeing he had touched a nerve he put a dusty boot on the white arm of the chair.

"Don't rightly know what I need. I do know what you need, and it's more than me. What you have is the worst kind of intruder, one who learns fast, hunts fast, and thinks fast. Seen only a few of these wipe out whole villages in a moment. They will probably start breeding soon, making this one big bowl of meat."

Precious didn't move, but paled slightly. "So what will you do?"

"My job, as always. But there are some things you need to do for me," Chris kept his voice neutral, much to Piers's relief.

"And they are?" ask Precious.

"One, I need a team of men, trained, armed and ready to respond to these things. Me and Marty can't fight them all at once. Two, I need somewhere to set up, and some kit from my stockpile. I will get that myself, while Marty starts training the men. Finally, I need to be left alone to do it all. No interference, no comments, no questions. It happens my way, or bye bye."

Precious made notes, then frowned. He had hoped this could vanish quickly, not make a small army, especially of these vagabonds.

"Leave it with me, Mr. Spencer," he said. Pressing a button on the huge dark wood desk the mayor began laboriously writing out notes while the Attendant opened the doors and led them all out. This time he didn't look apologetically at Piers, but almost scared. Piers liked that.

Outside Marty started to the car before he realised Chris had stopped just outside the door.

"Get my rifle," he told Marty, who went without comment and collected both his and Chris' weapons. Piers opened his mouth to speak, but one look from Marty killed the words in his throat. Chris smelt something, and he didn't like it. Taking his rifle he loaded it, put it to his shoulder and walked slowly, half stooped out the gates. The guards looked as puzzled as Piers, but kept out of the way of the two armed men. Piers followed out of curiosity.

Moving slowly down the smooth stone of the roadside walkway Chris looked very out of place in his woodland camouflage, something he mad a mental note to rectify as soon as he could. Marty followed, covering the rear in long, slow arcs of his rifle. Piers kept a little distance, fearful of distracting them. People in the street were nervous of two armed tramps walking the streets, but calmed when they saw Piers's uniform. Chris carried on towards the river, and the Main Bridge. Before he reached the stone cats he stopped, and dropped to one knee. Marty copied him, as did Piers. Chris raised one closed fist, then crawled forwards. By the parapet was a gap for people to walk the riverside. Few did as the smell of dried mud and sewage was unpleasant at the best of times. Chris smelt something else; blood.

The muddy bank had a rough stone path cut into the side so workers could get into the underground drains. These opened onto the shrunken river at several places, each about four feet in diameter. It was besides one of these Chris slid beside, taking a quick look inside, and sniffing. Marty leaned over the edge and saw Chris beside the drain, the mud below covered in three toed footprints like giant birds, with a rough scrape like drag marks. He was about to whistle for Chris when a shrill scream made them both jump. Chris scrambled up the bank, covered in stagnant mud. He took off at full sprint, which Marty struggled to follow, and Piers, who rarely had to run, fell behind.

There was a small group of people running from a tunnel entrance. Inside Chris heard moans of pain, and snarling. He stopped at the top of the stone steps long enough for Marty to catch up, then raised his rifle and stepped into the gloom. He saw by the dim light three forms on the floor, surrounded by waving tails. Tapping Marty he made a gesture of pulling a grenade pin. Marty shook his head, he had none either. Silently cursing Chris put his mouth to Marty's ear and whispered directions. By now Piers had caught up and watched in terrified awe as the two professionally went to work.

Chris stooped and went to the left side of the steps, moving silently. Marty went to the right side. They were only feet apart but the narrow tunnel prevented them moving more. The chamber the animals were eating in was actually a break between flights of steps, barely twenty feet square. The five dinosaurs were noisily crunching on the bodies, pausing to look around, blood dripping from pointed jaws. Neither saw the two men, with rifles constantly on them. Chris made a low click, telling Marty to stop. He went to one knee and aimed. Marty did the same. Piers clung to the rail that ran down the centre of the steps and watched. With one last glance at Marty, who nodded, Chris smiled. To Piers's horror Chris then shouted loudly. The dinosaurs stopped mid bite and all looked at the men. One snarled a high pitch wail that hurt Piers's ears. Chris was unaffected and fired.

The flash from the rifle, and the bang bounced around the cavern, rolling like thunder. Piers was blinded briefly, then Marty fired too. Both rifles bucked as fingers squeezed trigger. With all the smoke from the bullets it was hard to see the effect, but the higher pitched cry told of at least one down. When the scream stopped Chris whistled loudly. Both stopped firing. There was no wind to clear the smoke that smelt like stale bread. After an eternity the cavern was deserted, save the three bodies, and two dinosaurs. Chris kept his rifle up and walked bent low towards the two new bodies. He looked all around, then lay his rifle down beside the first, drew his knife from his belt, and cut the head off, struggling with the tough skin. Once done he decapitated both, then tucked one head under his right arm, and walked backwards to Marty, rifle held in one hand pointed back into the cavern. In the light of the street a large crowd had formed. Piers came out first, dusty, but alive, them Marty in his green and brown drab, and finally Chris, soaked in blood holding a giant dusty brown egg, only it wasn't an egg. Women screamed and fainted, men paled. The eyes were still open, the jaw hung limp, showing rows of jagged sharp teeth. Red blood dripped from the stump of a neck onto the worn stone. Chris held the head to Piers, who recoiled in horror. Marty watched the pantomime with interest. Chris was good at this bit. He watched as Chris held the head high with both hands to display the kill.

Unlike villages where this was met with cheers and whistles, the city people shrank back, pale and trembling. More women screamed, some men even vomited. Mildly confused Chris lowered the head, then absently tossed it to Marty, who couldn't help but wave it to Piers, who still looked terrified. Chris changed his rifles magazine for a full one, watched Marty change his, then walked back to the courtyard. the crow parted around him, keeping back just in case. Piers resisted the urge to stay and followed Marty, keeping that horrid head out of sight.

Chapter Six

The Attendant shrank from bloody mess Chris held, waving at the man like an identity pass as he walked through the waiting area. He went right into the mayors office without knocking. Precious was not at his desk, but on the arm chair. Two near naked young ladies were giggling on his lap before Chris burst in. They screamed and ran, more from shock than the sight of the head. Ignoring them Chris dropped the head on the mayors dark wood desk, smiled at him, and left. Precious didn't see him go. Only the sight of that snarling grin, pointed right at him, filled his world. He felt his bowels weaken, and bolted as best his bulk let him to the wash room.

Outside the Attendant still trembled, but Chris didn't care. He had won a major battle. He had shocked the mayor, who now knew there was something nasty out there, and he had to take it seriously. Life should be easier from now on. Downstairs Marty sat in the car waiting. Piers having self elected himself to their group, stood behind the big gun. Still smiling Chris got in.

"Where is our new home?" he asked Piers, turning in his seat to face the man.

"What new home? Had the mayor allocated you a place?"

"He will now," said Chris. "I need a decent, strong building, easily defended, secure and private. Where we can move into the city easily, but be out of the way."

Piers thought for a long time. Finally he brightened.

"There's the old storehouse by the river. It's just off the Main bridge, with a path to the Lesser Bridge. Stone walled, and I think a metal locking door there. Space on the roof too,"

"Perfect," said Chris, starting the car. "Lead on, boy."

Marty smiled. When Chris called people things like 'boy' he had accepted them. He liked Piers, even if he was from the soft city. He had guts and a hard edge inside. Chris would sharpen that. As they drove through the streets, people stopped and muttered to each other, Marty felt strangely at home. Maybe he lived here once before, maybe somewhere similar. Chris said there were other cities like this one around the land, but without any recollections before meeting Chris, Marty had no idea. Piers shouted lefts and rights as the river came closer. Before the bridge and the parapet Chris had climbed down to the river they turned left among large, plain stone building, windowless and walled in. Here was the area of the storehouses, where food and goods were held, before being distributed to the rich, or collected by the poor. Nearby the factories making tools, storage boxes and packing materials loomed with tall chimneys and clanking. As Piers had said their space was a vacant storehouse just off the main road liking the two bridges on the north side of the river. It was the same as the others, no open places, just walls and steel doors. Chris noted the corrosion on the rolling doors, another thing to fix. He also saw the roof was flat, like most were, but had a low wall built on it. Prefect for training people out of sight, and to sleep. Chris couldn't sleep under a roof, feeling too constricted. He liked the open.

Parking in the doorway Chris gestured for Marty to help him open the small metal door beside the roller door. With a scream it opened, letting the hot, musty air of the empty storehouse out. Before they went in both collected their rifles. Feeling like he should help out Piers waved to Chris, then tapped his hip. Chris paused, then drew his own pistol and held it out by the muzzle. Piers took the grip and looked at the battered black metal of the barrel. His eyes set and he followed the men inside. A quick check of the warehouse showed no signs of unwanted visitors, no holes or drains, and nothing left. Chris slung his rifle on his shoulder and rolled the door up. Marty kept his rifle ready, watching. He saw Piers taking a similar stance, holding the pistol with both hands. He would need to be shown how to hold it properly, but he could learn.

Chris drove the Land Rover inside, parking near the

steps to the roof. The steps ran up one side of the building, stopping only for an office area with big windows overlooking the storehouse. It was here Chris planned to store equipment, close by should they need it. He also needed a lot more from his cache in the bunker, but he would get that soon. He would need to leave Marty to prepare the storehouse and start inspecting volunteers.

"Piers," Chris called.

"Yes, sir?" Piers asked.

"Wanna come help me stock up? Be a few days outside, head to where I keep my stuff, get a trailer, head back. Maybe even teach you to drive, be better with two cars."

Piers looking like crying. "I would love to, Boss. When?"

"Now." Chris turned to Marty. "Take only what you need, stash the rest up there," he pointed to the office area. "Nobody comes in, nobody takes anything. Keep the door closed, stay hidden and do nothing. Clean up and be ready when I get back. I'll need a few trips so maybe if old Precious can loan us a truck or two would make life a lot easier, even though you can't get one of those near the bunker we can shuttle from there."

Marty nodded. "What if there's another attack?" he

asked.

"There will be," Chris said. "Loads. But without support and kit we can only get ourselves killed and I don't fancy that. If we have to face these things we do it our way, not theirs. Oil this damn door, clean up and be ready. And keep this all safe. Don't want them lot nicking anything."

Marty began pulling equipment off the car, Piers helped. Chris went to the roof and checked around. Plenty of room, plenty of options and no interference. Seemed too good to be true. Once the car was stripped to the minimum of what Chris felt was needed for the trip he said a brief farewell to Marty, got in the car and drove off. Marty felt a twinge of jealousy of Piers, in his seat, going away, but he knew they would be back soon. Life of a Hunter was exciting, but not always. With a sigh Marty closed the roller door, dug out a stiff bristled broom and began sweeping.

In the Land Rover Piers felt a thrill he had never known. Chris threw him a jacket and trousers from a small locker in the back, telling him he needed them. They were the same pattern as Chris and Marty's clothes. Piers stripped his clean uniform without shame and put the new clothes on. Feeling the rough fabric, firm boots and the dusty smell from the locker he saw in his minds eye a vision of himself, with his own Land Rover, roaming the plains, killing monsters, winning the love of villagers everywhere, being an equal with Chris and Marty.

He soaked up the looks and attention as the battered car rumbled through the streets to the west gate. He wished he had a pistol and holster on his hip like Chris, and the equipment belt, to finish the look. At the gate he even presumptuously waved away the guards and lookouts who asked for his papers. Chris suppressed a smile, and when asked for his identification he drew his pistol. The worn metal stopped the questions, and they were allowed to drive out.

On the dusty main road, rolling west over the undulating plains, Piers felt the wind in his short hair, the sun on his face, and a warmth in his heart. Chris drove in silence, a silence Piers swam in, dreaming of Piers, the great Hunter. They passed villages, large and small. Moving at a fast speed flies hurt when they hit his face. Chris had put on some goggles, and Piers looked around for some for himself.

"Box in front of you," Chris said. "Push the button."

Piers found the cubby box in front of him and pulled out a pair of goggles.

"How long have you been doing this?" he asked Chris.

"No idea. Too long. Many cycles."

"When did you start?"

Chris chuckled. "You gonna write a tale about me?" he asked.

"No," said Piers with alarm. "Just wondering."

"Well don't. Started young. Had a farm, went wrong. Village was attacked by a dino, I got away. Roamed some woods for food and found where we are going. Full of guns, ammo, food in bags that last forever, and loads of weird things."

"Such as?" asked Piers.

Chris took a deep breath. "Giant arrows that fire themselves, trucks without wheels with massive guns on the front, metal boxes with big blades on the top and sides, and massive metal birds."

Piers looked questioningly at Chris, then decided he wasn't lying. "How long until we get there?" he asked.

Chris thought for a bit, looked to the sun, high in the sky, and then the small dials in front of him.

"Maybe tonight if all goes well. We need to be there soon, low on fuel," he said.

Piers nodded and lapsed into silence again. Inside his dream of the super Hunter grew. Chris was also deep in thought, but on how he was going to do what he had said. He never broke a promise, if he did it was because he was dead. But to rid the city of a infestation of dinosaurs was not an easy task. It was bigger than anything he had done before. He realised he hadn't told Precious what it would cost him. Maybe the storehouse, another cache for him, a big one. But could he trust them? He thought of Marty, all alone it the big city. He could trust Marty, he had to. When your life depended on trust it became hard to break on both sides. But he couldn't trust that fat mayor. Best to get back quick. Maybe three days. Hopefully three days.

It was dark by the time Chris found the entrance to the bunker. The failing light made it harder in the trees and undergrowth to find the dirt track. He hid his relief as the familiar shape of the metal door loomed out of the dark. Stopping outside with the cars lights cast feeble shadows he drew his rifle, motioned Piers to stay put, and checked around. After a few minutes he had checked his traps for tampering, and decided it was undisturbed. He beckoned Piers over and together they lifted the heavy metal hatch to the door. Chris paused for a moment, unsure whether to let this guy know his secret, then decided he had to trust him. The car was on fumes and Marty was all alone in a city. With a heave he swung the door open. Darkness waited for them, cold and thick. Chris fumbled inside the doorway, and found the switch.

The larger metal screen door beside them creaked open electronically.

Chris drove the Land Rover inside, then shut both doors. He let Piers go in front, then hit the lights switches one after the other. Large bright lights clunked on way overhead. Piers stood awestruck.

They were standing in a conical chamber, the door as the narrow apex, fanning outwards from them. In one long line to their left stood more Land Rovers, trailers, larger trucks, strange metal boxes with rolls for wheels and long gun barrels, and at then end some sort of giant truck with arms on it. To the right was a long line of massive metal storage boxes, stacked two high each well over the height of a man. In front were several small windmills on their sides with wheels and seats, behind some metal birds with wings outstretched. Two giant metal birds, easily dwarfing everything, sat behind all this. Piers was still impressed with the lights. Electricity was rare in the city, some had made wind generators from lucky parts, but none had such as this.

Chris left him to stare and headed to the line of cars. He pulled an empty trailer away from the line, checked the tyres, and pushed it to the back of the Land Rover. He then got a flat metal trolley from beside the door and squeaked it to the containers on the right. Pulling out big metal boxes with yellow marking he loaded the trolley, and squeaked back to the trailer. Stacking the black boxes in the back her did another two trip to make sure it was full. Piers came over to help, dragged from his shock, and Chris set him to find the larger trailer bigger than the car. He found it hidden at the back, and grunted with effort to push it. Chris saw it had a flat tyre, so changed it.

"How come this place is so clean," Piers asked as Chris changed the wheel.

"Strange, ain't it?" Chris said. "Think those big boxes on the ceiling extract the dust and keep it clean and dry. Most of this stuff is far older then the tech manuals I've found say they should last. Well preserved. The fuel should have gone off, but it's been treated and sealed. Still a bit iffy sometimes, why the car smokes." Chris chucked the wheel brace into the trailer's tool box and stood. "Speaking of cars; driving lesson." For the next two hours he tried to teach Piers how to drive, before exhaustion overtook both of them. Chris found Piers a hammock, showed him how to string it, then they both fell asleep.

The next day Chris was up early, sorting through the mountains of equipment. He had decided to use one of the trucks he had to load his Land Rover, plus two others, and hitch another trailer to that with equipment on. Piers would drive another truck loaded with fuel. With all that loaded the bunker looked no less empty.

Happy he had all he needed they left, Chris paused to make sure his traps were set. It took longer to get back, loaded as they were, and Piers struggled with his heavy truck. The fuel trailer holding him back. It wasn't until the fourth day since leaving Marty, in the morning, they returned to the city. Chris had insisted they drive through the night. The gate didn't want to let them in, but when Chris threatened to remove the gate himself they did. He told Piers to stay with his truck, and drove the bigger one to the storehouse. Marty, his equipment and weapons were nowhere to be seen.

Parking the truck inside Chris did his best to seal the storehouse, then ran to the west gate. Piers caught his worried expression, but couldn't get an answer until Chris had his breath back, and even then it was clipped, and impolite. They dropped off the other truck, then Chris ordered Piers to keep watch, and shoot anyone who came unless it was him or Marty. Then he stormed off, rifle in his hand, to the governors court.

Ignoring the pleadings of the Attendant Chris put one dusty boot to the white door, sending it flying. Before the mayor could do anything Chris was in, rifle to his shoulder, barrel against Precious' nose.

"Where is he, Tubs?" Chris threatened.

"W-w-who?" stammered Precious.

"You know w-w-who, you great fat owl. Marty is who

who. Where is he?"

Agent Parks watched proceedings with a mixture of amusement and horror. He had one of the few pistols in the city, kept secret under the black robe, but at no point did he attempt to get it. He sat back in the armchair and watched.

"I d-don't know," said Precious. "Where did you leave him?"

"You know, fatty, and you had him taken. Now he's gone, his kit is gone, and soon you'll be gone out of the bloody window so best be telling me now," Chris smelt the sweat on the man, the fear. He was tired, dirty and angry. Not the best combination. Precious saw the rage in his eyes and visibly sagged.

"He was taken to the internment area. He was a threat to our citizens."

"A threat? If he was a threat what am I?" Chris snarled.

"I'm not sure," said Precious, trying to regain some composure. "Depends what you do now."

Chris half smiled, which to Precious was worse. "That depends on what you do now. If he isn't back at the storehouse by the river, with everything he had, and an apology I'll go get him myself, and the deal is off."

Precious tried to speak but Chris had already left, the Attendant peeped nervously around the door, to be waved away by Precious. Parks leant over and pushed the door closed.

"It seems our Mr Spencer is a loyal man," Parks said in his high voice, inspecting the boot print on the white door.

"He's a nuisance. I should never have listened to you, Agent Parks," said Precious, mopping his brow with a handkerchief. "There will be trouble, mark my words."

"There always is, Precious," said Parks, and stood. "If there is to be trouble, I had better investigate it." He nodded and left, opening the door for himself. Precious felt a shudder after the agent had gone, and began to wish he hadn't been so prosperous.

Chapter Seven

Marty was dropped by a buggy five minutes after Chris got back. Piers kept his distance, letting Chris pull out some of the black boxes and sliding green tubes from them. When Marty smiled around the door Chris dropped the tubes and ran to him. He held him in his arms for a long time, then slapped him hard.

"What the hell?" Marty asked, wiping blood from his lip.

"Don't get caught. Golden rule. What the hell happened?"

Marty pulled his kit in, noting how much Chris had brought.

"I was biding my time when someone knocked at the door," Marty said. "Had loads of knocks, asking to help, or for it. Some asked me to leave, others to come eat with them. Turned them all down. Then this pretty young thing knocked."

Chris groaned and turned away. He should have guessed.

"Well," Marty continued, "couldn't leave here out here all alone, and it was dark, so said to come in, sleep here, then go home in the morning. When I went to sleep I was woken by a load of men trying to break in. She screamed and ran for the door, letting them in. Seems her dad didn't like my kindness." Marty smiled and showed his bruised eye.

"So then what?" Chris asked. "How do a bunch of weaklings overpower you?"

"Simple matter of numbers. They already had me pinned, then the Law turned up. They said I was attacking the girl, and dragged me away. The fat mayor and his black buddy tried asking me questions, but they didn't like my story."

"Check your kit," said Chris, and left him to it while he unloaded the trucks. Piers drifted over, pleased Chris' anger seemed vented.

"Got in a bit of trouble then?" Piers asked.

"Trouble?" replied Marty. "Thought they were gonna beat me to death. Think if it wasn't for the deal with Chris they would have."

Piers shook his head. "There is no death punishment. You would have been stripped, dressed in rags and sent out the south gate, your face on all the gates denial boards, and never allowed back in."

"At least it's all here," said Marty, going through his pack, the equipment left behind and some extras Marty had claimed when he was released. This included some fresh meat that he started cooking on a solid fuel burner. Chris smelt it, and suppressed his anger.

"You're supposed to be helping, not cooking," he growled from behind the trucks.

"Aw, boss. Come eat, and sleep. You get real grumpy when you're tired," Marty pleaded, wafting the smell of the meat Chris' way.

Chris appeared, took a tin and ate.

"Only because I don't waste food," he said. After, he and Piers slept while Marty stood guard.

A deputation of very unimpressive men waited outside the metal door to the storehouse the following morning. Marty had let Chris and Piers sleep as long as he could, but the polite threats left him little choice. He went to wake Chris.

"Huh?" murmured Chris, still wrapped in his sleeping bag in the office over the storehouse. "Wassup, Marty?" He half rolled, half fell out of bed, hitting the wooden floor hard. He grabbed his rifle and stood ready, then realised Marty was unarmed. Not an emergency then.

"Trouble," Marty said. "Got a load of blokes outside saying they want to see you. Now."

Chris grunted, cuffed the sleep from his eyes and looked to the sun. He was indoors so had no idea of the time.

"Mid afternoon," Marty said.

"Huh," said Chris, and ambled downstairs. Outside the crowd had grown noisier. Chris decided against opening the front door, and headed back upstairs to the roof. He leant over the edge, about forty feet from the ground. There was about twenty men, of various ages, waiting by the metal roll door. All had some sort of weapon, most were bits of furniture.

"There he is," one shouted, pointing upwards. The rest started calling out in such a din Chris couldn't understand what they were saying. He held both hands out to stop them.

"What's this all about, then?" he asked.

"We want to join you," said the man who had spotted him, self elected spokesman.

"Join me?" Chris laughed. "Join yourself. You ain't got what it takes."

"Yeah?" called another. "You think?" a third. Chris held his hands out again.

"Ok," he said. "You drop those stupid toys and try to get past Marty. He'll open the door and one at a time you can have a go. You get in, you're in." Marty gave Chris a dirty look, then tramped downstairs. Chris turned back to the crowd.

"Who's first then?" he called. The men pulled each other back to get to the front. Marty opened the metal hinged door and stepped out. He had a pistol in his hand, held ready. Most of the men turned and tried to get away, a couple stepped aside. Three stood still, then stepped forwards. They saw Marty didn't move so kept walking forwards until they passed him and went inside. The others, feeling they had lost the test tried to follow, but when Marty cocked his pistol they checked. Chris laughed again.

"I need men with guts, and balls. Come back when you have some." He turned from their shouts and headed inside. Piers was still snoring, so Chris left him. Downstairs Marty had locked the door, and the three men stood uncertainly in the gloom.

"Why did you three walk past Marty?" Chris asked.

"Well," said the first, "I didn't think he would shoot us, not without reason."

"Were you scared?" Chris asked.

"Yes," said the man after a pause.

Chris turned to the next. "You?"

The man dropped his head. "Yes," he whispered.

The third already bowed his head and just nodded. Chris took a few steps, then spoke loudly, and with authority.

"Never be ashamed of fear. It's there to help you. Use it wisely. You have proved you have courage. That means you have accepted your fear, and overcome it. I need people who can face that fear, beat it, and do what is needed. You three have it. If you want it, and will work for it, then you are in. But it won't be easy."

The men didn't flinch, but looked at Chris attentively. Marty had seen this side of him before, usually when villagers decide the asking price was too much.

"I have been hunting things that hunt you for years. I trained Marty here, I have lived. I still live. And to make sure I still live I need those I can trust around me. If you run away, I die. And if you stand and fight, we live. If you can't stand, if you want to run like a girl, then leave before we waste my time and yours."

Piers shuffled as quietly as he could down the steps. He was still in his camouflage with no equipment belt. Chris didn't move, but seemed to know Piers was there.

"All four of you will train with me and Marty. It will be tough, exhausting, and complicated." The men looked around at Marty, Piers, and the mean looking trucks and cars around them. There was a glint forming in their eyes. Chris noted it with interest.

Chris took his rifle from Marty, cocked it, and fired at the ceiling. The noise was amazing, and the muzzle flash briefly lit the large space. Chris didn't look away from the men, who jumped, but that was all.

"First test passed," Chris announced. "Time for part two. Marty; some running I think. Everyone line up with Marty, that means you too Piers." Chris had spotted Piers trying to slink back to the steps unseen. With a small shrug of irritation he joined the others.

For the next week Chris had Marty run them ragged. They slept on the floor with only a blanket and their own clothes to sleep on. They ran laps of the storehouse inside and out. They ran through the thick mud of the riverbank, through the streets, even doing a lap of the walls. All done with Marty behind. All wore the camouflage clothing issued, a mark of authority and respect, Chris said. They ran with large packs on their back, sweat pouring down their faces. Everyday the weight increased. Chris tried to break them, and to their credit they stood firm. In the evenings when they were tired he made them form two lines inside, facing each other. Stripped naked they had to wrestle each other, the overall winner had less weight the next day. As the week passed Chris saw what he wanted. They were working as a group, pushing each other, supporting each other. Marty tried his best to break them too. He knew the risk of someone scared with you. Accidents, and the risk of desertion were lethal threats. He didn't want that risk, so tried to force them to quit. They didn't.

After the first week Chris allowed them some time off exercise to learn how to fight. They started with small blades and knives, then the rifle knife that fitted over the barrel, then after three weeks they were introduced to the rifle properly. Chris secured a clear patch of the riverbank and they stood in line on the other side shooting at wooden boxes in front of the mud. After only a few days the number of holes in the mud dropped, and the holes in the wood increased. In the storehouse the equipment was organised to one wall, vehicles to another, sleeping in between and training all over. More men tried to join, but only a few passed the 'Marty' test and they were made to run like the first group, by the newly promoted Piers. After two months Chris decided the first ten men were ready to begin patrols of the city, and another twelve were nearing readiness. Outside the death toll kept rising. The tunnels and drains were abandoned, and a dusk curfew helped reduce casualties, but some were snatched in their homes, some at work, some even in daylight. Precious kept the pressure on Chris, who ignored the endless stream of messengers sent from the fat mayors office. He needed time to make them ready. And soon they would be.

Chapter Eight

The heat grew as the cycles passed. It was like no previous summer Chris could remember, and even the elder inhabitants were surprised how warm it became. The sunlight ricochet off the off white walls, baking the streets below. Dark corners were hard to find, but the man waiting was impressed how his contact had found this one. Near the river, but away from the underground pipes, this was unused, empty, and silent. He waited for the allotted time, his pocket timer clicking was the only sound he heard. The walls were smooth, this corner seemed forgotten by the builders, a unusual waste of space. The man kept looking towards the entrance, the only way in or out of the smooth, windowless area. He nearly screamed when the voice spoke.

"Are you alone?" it asked, squeaky and distorted.

"Yes," said the man, looking around.

"Good," said the voice. The man didn't like how it spoke. Made his teeth itch. "You are to report here every week without fail, at this time. No excuses. I need to know everything."

"Such as what?" asked the man, still looking.

"How many he has with him, where he sleeps, what equipment he has, how much, if he snores. I don't care, just everything."

"What's in it for me?" asked the man.

The voice took a new, darker tone. "Your life, your wife and daughters lives, and your brothers life," it said.

The man paled. "Ok," he said. "I'll do it. Who are you?"

"Nobody," said the voice.

"Why do you want to know?" asked the man. The

voice was silent. After a nervous wait the man decided it wasn't going to speak, and left. In the dark corner the wall moved, was shaken out and rolled up. A man in black put the roll under his arm and left.

Chris was pleased with the first recruits, so much so he decided to promote them. Piers was a natural leader, and the other three were of the same build. Don Helfer was the oldest recruit, with three teenage kids, wife and a larger sized flat in the richer part of the poor sector. His sister had been killed in the first major public attack, when Piers was patrolling the marketplace. He had a desire to see the creatures killed, and a flair for planning. He became Chris' third. Edgar Phipps was a lot younger, and cleverer. He had a small family, and was very close to them all. He had on of the quickest reactions Chris had ever seen, being able to master hand to hand fighting, and usually winning the fights Chris had the recruits perform. His ability to learn quickly, and retain what he learned made him stand out, and his loyalty was impressive. Pete Aarons was a lot quieter, but had a hard edge when he let it out. Chris was going to drop him when he showed signs of being too timid and shy. The fights changed him, and though still withdrawn, when his blood was up he was unstoppable. He had a nose for the job, and when Chris started them on tracking training, letting Marty go ahead in the open grass areas near the government courtyards, Pete was the one who found the trail first. He was Chris' new scout, a man he knew could find their target.

After three months worth of training Chris gathered all the recruits, under their new sectional leaders, and sat them in front of one of the blank walls. He had a stack of paper drawings he had spent many days working on. One by one he had Marty hold them up as Chris talked.

"Ok, kids, settle. Settle! Oi! Shuttup! Thank you so much. Now, this is 'know your enemy' time. You are about ready to go out. Some have gone, but they won't come back. You who are here are in. you made it. Well done, pat yourself on the back, smile, shake hands lah di dah and all that. So. What are we dealing with? Let me tell you a tale. Millions of cycles ago some pretty nasty things lived here."

"Eddy's brother?" asked one, to a roar of laughter. Edgar gave him a friendly punch.

"Not his brother, although I see where you are coming from," said Chris. "Nope, these were massive eating machines made to catch their food. They hunted, smaller ones in packs, larger ones alone. They breed like birds, laying eggs, which they guard. They don't fly, but they can run faster than us. They have claws, and teeth, and all manner of nasty tricks. They kill for the fun, to store for later, or just because it moved. They know if they fail they die. They won't give up easily. Be aware they are hard to kill, and near impossible to trick."

Chris waved a metal bar at the first drawing Marty held up.

"This is one of the bigger monsters you have to face. Doubt you will see one here, but you never know. It's called Allosaurus, that's it's official name. I call them Allys and they are about four to five times your height, powerful and best disposed off with a rocket tube."

Marty lifted the next picture.

"This is more common, again not likely here. It's a bit smaller than the Allys, but still formidable. This tough bugger is called a Troodon, and likes munching small livestock like goats or kids. Again a good hit with a tube will take it's ugly head off. Next we have what we have here, called Deinonychus. It's about your height, nimble as a spider, tough as a wall and smarter than you lot. One rifle bullet to the head and it will just get mad. Bone in the head is thicker than Dave's there," Chris pointed to one recruit who actually blushed, making the jeers worse.

"Anyway," continued Chris, "these things are pack Hunters. Strong, sharp, tough. They can smell you, hear you, sense you long before you know they are there. They stink like your feet but still smell you first. Dark brown like dried blood they are hard to see in darkness, and run faster then I can drive. Only time I have faced them in a tight spot was here with Marty, and that was using grenades."

Chris lifted his rifle to show a new attachment. This was a fat short tube under the barrel.

"This lovely thing here is a grenade launcher. Now, my plan to find these things is to systematically close the tunnels, one by one, until they are trapped. Then we set traps with the bang boxes, lure them there with some freshly killed animal, and smash them."

Marty watched the silent men as they soaked up all they heard. There was no doubts in their eyes, no murmurs of complaint. They all knew what was expected, and they wanted to do it. Marty had his own doubts on the venture. They had no plans of the tunnels, they would have to go through them as a group and hope the sheer size of numbers would be enough. Even then it was doubtful. Also they hadn't found out where these things were coming in, even after a visual search by Chris and Marty of the walls from outside. Who knew what was down there? Chris knew from his search of the mysterious lab years ago what was bred there, but that was a thankfully short list of herbivores, and three carnivores. But Marty was painfully aware that was only the pictures Chris found they had done. There could be anything roaming out there. Or under their feet. Chris was still talking, about plans to form into two large groups, but Marty couldn't focus. He felt numb, almost separate. The cold metal of his rifle barrel, heavy in his grip, felt reassuring. They had faced all kinds of dangers, both human, modern and prehistoric, and come out fine.

Why was he worried?

"So, grab some sleep, prep your kit and be ready," Chris said, waving them away. He glanced at Marty, saw how wobbly he looked, but left him alone. He went to his own hammock to sleep.

Over the following week they practised with the grenade launchers, getting used to running with the weapons, firing, and patrolling the storehouse area in small teams. They felt the suspicion of the city folk, but also the slow realisation that they were there to help, and slowly were accepted. This continued presence meant they were looked at as a saviour, not a criminal, almost revered. Gifts of clothing, food and ancient weapons were regularly left at the door. In the streets people would ask them into their homes for food and talk. Chris began to find he missed the plains less than he used to, almost feeling wanted here like he did before. After the initial scepticism he had received from the prettily dressed residents he was now almost a celebrity. The papers wanted interviews, even woodcut pictures of him for their latest news. Recruits hoping to join sometimes made a line back to the river, waiting patiently to be told to go home, no space. All the time the threat from below kept reminding those above it was still there. Cellars were forced open and people snatched in their own beds. The dinos grew braver, sometimes stalking the night darkened streets for late walkers and security patrols. Chris felt forced by Precious to start nightly patrols, although he told them not to attack anything, to stay in the well lit areas, and to only report any incident, not be involved. They saw nothing. Over three months since they started training the recruits were ready. Chris had the lined up in the storehouse.

"Ok, listen in," he said, calling their attention. "Tomorrow we go down below, start searching for the nest. Don, and Eddie, your two groups will come with us. Pete? You're group stay here and keep an eye on this, and maintain routine patrols, but be on stand by. We will take two cars with kit. Four will stay with them to keep watch. One other car will be outside here with four guards, ready in case we need support. Take only ammo and grenades. You know how to use it all, so don't be filling your pouches too full. I will take a patrol from Pete's group later today to see the main tunnel by the main bridge. Just to have a sniff. Feel something there and I don't like it. Pete, you're with us too. Need your nose. Marty will wait on support back here, car outside ready to go. Get your kit sorted and get some sleep. Pete? Need eight of your best and you for this walk, rifles and grenades only. Travel light. Get to it people."

Chris hefted his rifle, then checked it again. Pete had his rifle in parts already, checking and oiling the moving parts. He shouted the selected names and those men also did their preparations. Marty hovered around Chris.

"Say your piece," Chris said looking at his rifle bolt.

"Why without me?" Marty asked.

"Because, if anything goes wrong I need you to carry on. These guys can handle a little reconnaissance job. Smell something big down there. Something new."

"All the more reason to take me, boss," said Marty. "Someone with experience.

"You never keep all your food in one place," said Chris, refitting the bolt. "You stay here. If we need help we'll call."

Marty didn't look pleased, but he knew Chris was right. His words haunted him though. 'Something big' he had said. Yet he only went in with rifles. Clearly Chris didn't mean to come to a conflict, but to go under prepared was not his style. Still concerned Marty went to the car Chris was using, and slid two rocket tubes into the back. Chris didn't notice, and as he drove out into the brilliant sun outside the mass of men clinging onto the Land Rover hid them.

"Piers," called Marty. "Get a group together, take a car and wait for Chris if he need you. Eddie, pick five and be ready to follow me. Patrol time."

"What area?" asked Edgar.

"Near the main bridge," said Marty. He had Chris'

back for years. He was damned if he was going to leave him now.

In the bright afternoon sun the tunnel still loomed dark like a stone lined rabbit hole. A smell like rotten meat and faeces drifted from the depths. Chris parked the car near the bridge, and gathered the group around him.

"Ok, listen. Pete, you go last, keep our asses covered. I'll go first. Cover yours arcs, keep silent. Anything unusual I miss tap the guy in front. Don't shoot without something definite to hit, and keep your cool. We're being watched and those nice girls don't like a fool." Chris smiled as some of the men nervously looked at the growing crowd. Agent Parks was there, standing out in his dark robe, looking amused. Chris felt uncomfortable for a reason he couldn't place. A last check of their weapons, and three chosen to watch the car, and Chris led them slowly into the tunnel.

The stone steps were dusty from lack of use, and as his eyes acclimatised to the darkness Chris saw they were criss crossed with three toed tracks, some large, some tiny. Hatchlings. Lovely, Chris thought. Makes the adults more defensive. They crept slowly down the steps to the first level. Here the tunnel split two ways, one to the north roughly down more stone steps, the other south with some old shop fronts long abandoned beside them. It was only a small area, but made a perfect killing area.

Easy in, easy out. Small bones littered the floor. Maybe a feasting area, thought Chris, and motioned the men to wait while he checked. The area stank from the multiple piles of dropping left behind, and the lingering smell of rotten meat. One corpse that could have been human lay in a corner. Chris checked it, and very slowly looked down the north steps. He saw nothing. He crossed at a stoop to the southern steps and also saw nothing. Unsure which way to go he noticed the prints in the dust were mostly on the northern side. He waved the group forwards and headed down the northern steps. Feeling the tension in the air, sweat beading on his forehead, Chris kept his eyes peeled for anything, taking slow breaths through his nose with his mouth open to minimise noises he made to disturb his own sense of hearing.

With rifles to their shoulders the men felt they were finally part of something. The training, the effort, the mental and physical strain had all lead to this. They were defending their homes, their families and neighbours. They were invincible. The power of their weapons proved they could not be stopped. They walked with stealth, but also with confidence, hoping their prey would walk into their gun sights to be killed like animals. Only Chris felt apprehension of a survey patrol. When he knew where is quarry was he felt happier. Now it could be anywhere.

At the bottom of the steps was a much larger cavern,

with circular tunnels leading off in pairs on either side of what looked like a loading area. Steps had been fitted to allow easier walking from the raised platform. Footprints covered the floor in a mad pattern only made from prolonged passings. They checked the area, feeling the breeze from the white walled tunnels, and the horrible smell they brought. The men started to feel uncomfortable. Their original confidence was weakened by the smell, and the feeling of being out of their comfort zone. This was a place they had used regularly, the light that dimly lit the familiar features came from vents in the ceiling letting pools of light fall. Chris felt a tap on his shoulder and knelt down, checking around him. Behind him the men were doing the same. Pete came over to Chris and put his mouth to Chris' ear.

"Something is wrong," he breathed. Chris nodded. He felt it to. He rarely felt fear, especially on a hunt, but this felt wrong, badly wrong. He knew they were smart, but to leave guards?

Softly, like the breeze they heard to soft snort. A gentle hiss and a click of bone on stone made them all look frantically around. Chris decided they were spotted and flicked a flare from his belt. it's harsh light lit the cavern instantly. They all took one look and ran.

The roar of the dinosaur, in the enclosed, smooth tunnels echoed around them bouncing from wall to wall until it sounded like a hundred were behind them. The thumping of the ground with every giant step was lost in the noise of that massive roar. They ran up the steps three at a time, rifles on slings, just running. This was no organised withdrawal, this was a sprint for survival. Chris heard a grunt and then a scream. One man had fallen in the dark. The snapping of bones in the giant jaws made them all cringe.

Once inside the steps they felt safer, the ceiling was only a foot above their heads, and seemed solid. They still ran to the exit though, but were letting the reality sink in. soon they were on the smaller floor lit by the entrance. Slipping on faeces and bones they ran to the steps. A massive thud behind, with a billowing of dust did nothing to slow them down.

Marty saw the three guys Chris had left guarding the car, and decided to casually chat to them. He was trying to draw out the chat, running out of things to say, when he heard a roar like none he had heard before. Marty knew the noises these things made. The smaller ones almost screamed, the larger ones had chest space so they rumbled like a large boulder on a stony path. This was larger than anything before. Then they heard a scream and the snapping of twigs. Marty knew it wasn't twigs. He motioned his patrol to follow and raised his rifle. At the entrance he turned to see only half had followed. A thud, and dust drifted like smoke from the entrance, obscuring it. Marty nearly screamed as something ran out and flattened him. Lying on the floor he instinctively fought it until it shouted to stop. He realised it was Chris, and couldn't suppress the joy he felt, hugging him. Chris shrugged him of and ran. Marty knew long ago if Chris ran, you kept up with him. Picking up his rifle he followed.

The groups joined behind the car looking nervous. Chris slid in beside them, Marty soon after.

"What was it, boss?" Marty asked. Chris just panted and shook his head.

The men all looked terrified, eyes fixed on the dark entrance. Dust still rolled out, as did a rattling growl. One man stood, trying to be brave. Before Chris could stop him he raised his rifle and fired a grenade into the entrance. The small bomb blew the stonework apart, making a large ragged hole. The roar fired back, making them duck and the people watching turn and flee. Chris slapped the man down and spat dust.

"Damn it!" he cursed. "That was something new and too bloody big. We go back."

"What was it?" asked Marty.

"Damned if I know. Not on their list, but it's too big for us." Chris stopped, although had he continued he wouldn't have been heard. The shattered entrance exploded as the dino inside smashed its way free. Standing about thirty feet tall, with a massive head half the size of the car it blinked in the bright sunlight. The men cringed from the sight. Blood dripped from scrapes on its back, and from the savage jaws. Chris started searching the back of the car, knowing he was in plain sight. Some raised their rifles, but Marty waved them down. Chris had a rifle but chose not to use it. That must mean they wouldn't do anything. He waited impatiently for Chris to find the rockets.

The new dino shook it's head, saw Chris and roared. He ignored the noise and the thump of it's feet on the stone floor, still rummaging. Sensing their leaders defeat some men fired anyway. Chris scowled at them but it was too late. With the small stings from the bullets the dinosaur roared in rage and stormed the car. It flipped onto it's side, spilling equipment and men. Placing one foot on the side the dino dropped it's head and pulled on a man who was trapped. With a sickening tearing noise it pulled him free, leaving both his feet in their boots under the car. Blood was everywhere. Chris, thrown by the car, found one of Marty's tubes, aimed, then paused. The dino had the man screaming from its mouth by his arm. He swung slowly like a marionette waiting for the audience. Finally it dropped the man and opened it's jaws for the next. The rocket, hurriedly aimed, hit it in the ribs, exploding inside and flinging shreds of meat all over. The head looked confused for a brief moment, then the body lost strength as the blood flowed and it toppled sideways. The man still screamed.

Having heard the explosions the relief car slid to a stop next to the other car, men already picking up the injured comrade, and throwing him in the back they rushed to the medical area. Chris knew there was no hope for the man, and felt sad for him. Two lost to this thing.

As the men pushed the car onto its wheels and cleared up Chris inspected his kill. It was similar to an Allosaurus, but bigger, and tougher. The rocket had hit it in the chest, and exploded somewhere in its lungs. But the body around it was still fairly intact. The stomach was exposed and Chris saw some camouflaged cloth in the gore. When the car was sorted he ordered everyone back to the storehouse and tried to plan his next move. In the dark of the tunnel three sets of cold eyes watched them go, then turned and left with a flash of long, stiff tails.

Chapter Nine

The first rains came that evening, pouring with a desire to wash away the earth below. It ran in shallow rivers down the stone streets into the now swollen river.

The blood from the big kill diluted into the pale stones, making the dark stain lighter, but wider. The remains had quickly been cleared away by officials before the crowds could be scared any more by the grisly sight. Water burbled down the dark stone steps and into the murk of the tunnels. Nobody walked the streets, even the patrols had stopped. So nobody saw the two figures moving stealthily through the thick rain.

Chris lead, moving fast to the tunnel entrance. Marty followed. It was Chris' idea to go into the tunnels when the rain was coming down, the sound of the water, the smells and movement would give them an advantage finally. They knew they were out there, in the driving rain, when no prey was likely to travel. Travelling light, only rifle, some small explosives and flash grenades, they ran to the tunnel entrance, rifles raised ready. They saw nothing, and could hardly see anything anyway with the sheeting water. They found the kill site, the wrecked stonework now clean from the washing. The rain fell so hard it hurt. Chris paused by the low wall, then slipped inside. Marty kept his eyes peeled into the rain, then followed.

It was cold in the tunnel. The steps were slippery and the chilly breeze was more noticeable being wet from the rain. They crept through the flat area, water swirling around their feet. Down the northern stairs they crept, beside the smashed shops where the big thing had come from, and into the darkness. They let their eyes acclimatise to the dark, then carried on. Now it was all slow and silent. They breathed open mouthed, slow and deep. They even swallowed with their mouths open. Eyes scanned for a flash of movement, a glint of something, the blur of shadow. Ears strained to pick up any sound other than their own heavily beating heart. Although he wouldn't admit it, this was Chris at his happiest. The hunt was pure adrenaline. Kill, or be killed. If he did he job right he would walk out a hero, fail and he wouldn't walk out again ever. Marty felt sweat begin to form, even with the cold.

Pausing on the raised platform Chris waited for what seemed like eternity. They both kept looking around, searching for signs of their quarry. They knelt in shallow rain water running down the steps. Eventually Chris motioned to one of the dark circular tunnels. He must have smelt something. Almost back to back they walked through, avoiding the metal bars running parallel down the centre. Here stank of rotten meat and flies. Ignoring the deep down voice screaming to turn back they pressed on.

Chris froze, making Marty nearly fall over him. He slowly dropped to the floor like he was sleeping. Marty knew he had sighted his target. It could only be the nest. A dim glow lit the chamber ahead. Moving on his belly, making as little noise as possible, Chris scuffed forwards until he could see into the chamber. Lit from above by some unseen light was a massive cavernous area, bigger than four storehouses. Their tunnel joined it from one side, partially obscured by a collapsed section. From their concealed viewpoint Chris could see the nest. It was huge! Dozens of adult dinosaurs paced mounds of earth the same colour as the riverbed. Around them hundreds of infants of various heights ran, bounced, fought and slept. There had to be over three hundred in total. To one side large carcasses of dinosaurs, some Chris recognised, were piled. The area was protected by sentries, placed all around to watch the entrances. Water poured from cracks in the ceiling, making a roaring waterfall near Chris and Marty. It stank of sewage. Realising their weapons would have no chance of stopping the sheer number of animals Chris tapped Marty's leg, and they headed back.

Once in the rain again Marty started to relax. They kept silent still, keeping watch around them, but moved back a little slower then they had come. The storehouse suddenly didn't seem quite so safe. As they neared the river they saw how full it was becoming. The smell of sewage flushed from the drains was hardly watered by the humid air. As the storehouse formed in the downpour Chris new instinctively something was wrong. He began to run, spurring Marty to keep up. The door was forced open, the equipment gone, their men as well. Nothing remained, not even a scrap of paper. For a moment Chris wondered if they had the wrong one, easy to do in the rain. Marty shook his head and gestured to a mark on a wall from an accidental firing of a rifle. It was the right place, so where were they?

Chris sat in the empty doorway of the storehouse. Marty had searched and found the place picked clean. How could they all be gone? Chris asked himself. There were guards on the door, the roof and inside. There was little blood so it had to be men who took them. Only one man would be bold enough, and able to bluff his way in. Chris rose and walked back into the rain. Marty watched him go. That slow, deliberate walk from Chris who usually moved like his life depended on it, meant only one thing: trouble. He could stay, let Chris deal with it himself, and to follow would bring only a strong rebuke from Chris, but he was his mentor, his leader and his friend. Shrugging his rifle on his shoulder Marty followed.

He caught up with Chris at the mayors courtyard gates. They were closed, and the guards were hidden. Chris inspected them briefly then walked away. Marty waited for him to vanish into the dark rains, but after a few paces he stopped, turned and sprinted at the gates. With a full body slam they flew open, spilling Chris onto the wet stones. He rolled and was up and running before the gates bounced off the walls and began to close. Screaming a cry of rage Chris went straight for the mayors office, taking the outside door off it's hinges, pounding the stairs and through the double white doors into the office. It was empty. Kicking the side door open without trying the handle Chris searched the ornate bathroom. Nothing. Turning from the desk Chris was about to leave when he saw Marty. He had a look of apology on his face Chris rarely saw. It was a pure 'sorry, I screwed up big time this time' look. Checking his rage Chris saw the hand on the younger man's arm. Two guards appeared, followed by the black robed figure of Parks. He was smiling. The mayor nervously joined them from the stairs.

"Well, Mayor Precious," said Parks, voice dripping with smugness, "it seems we have an intruder. This man forced his way into an official building, damaging doors and furniture, and seems intent on murder. Whatever should we do with him?"

Precious tried to look imposing, but still looked scared. "That, Agent Parks, is a crime punishable with expulsion."

"Which, Mayor Precious, is carried out at dusk, wearing only rags and no possessions." Parks waved four guards in. "Strip them."

The guards looked nervously to the two men, one already in manacles, and hesitated. Only the threatening look for Parks made them move. They were more scared of him than Chris. It took all four to hold Chris down while Parks himself knelt and tore the uniform from

Chris' screaming, writhing body. Naked they left him on the floor and attacked Marty. Once the two men were manacled and clothed in two large, rough sacks they were carried out into the rain and down to a waiting buggy. Chris didn't stop shouting all the way.

Piers Compton felt only the weight of the cloth, the cold metal on his wrists, and shame. He had been sleeping with most of the team and woken only by a rough sack thrown over his head, and a hit that sent sparks in front of his eyes for minutes. Somehow the whole group must have been taken, and nobody fought back. They were dragged into the rain, instantly soaking the sack, then into a buggy of some kind. A long drive where he lost his bearings, then he was dropped onto the hard floor and dragged down some steps into a cold room. He heard moans so others must be there. He tried calling out, but his jaw felt locked from the hit. Forced into silence he tried to work out what Chris would have done. He decided Chris would not be in that situation and tried to work out what he should do. With no inspiration he slumped down and felt like crying.

Low voices made him raised his head. He couldn't understand them, but they were getting louder. Hands grabbed him roughly and lifted him to his feet. He played weak and kept trying to drop back down. A kick changed his mind and he shuffled with his captors. Led through narrow corridors, their feet echoing, he was turned left and right until he was lost again. Finally he was pushed into a chair, and the sack pulled off. He blinked in the sudden light.

"Greeting, Officer Compton," said a decidedly unfriendly voice. Piers focused his eyes, and screamed.

Parks waited patiently for Piers to stop screaming. The effect, he admitted, worked well. Several skulls from different species, some human, adorned his high wooden chair. Chemical lights blazed into the accused eyes while deep red lights lit the room. On the battered table between them lay a large selection of metal blades, different shapes and sizes, all designed to inflict pain. Parks had replaced his black robe with a cloak made from human skins, some with faces still clear.

"Done?" he asked as Piers paused to get his breath. Before he could scream again a man from behind put his hand over Piers's mouth. "Enough of that, Compton. I'm not here to torture you, although I would like too." Parks smiled evilly, his high pitched voice making it more menacing. Piers tried to keep calm but the stories of this room, to pain, the cries, filled him with terror. He felt warmth in his lap and actually blushed with shame.

"Oh dear," said Parks at the dampness. "Do I really scare you that much?"

Piers nodded, still unable to speak.

"If the nice man takes his hand away you won't scream any more? I would like a nice chat."

Piers nodded again. The hand released it's grip and Piers blew out his cheeks to try and shake the feeling off.

"What do you want, Agent Parks?" he asked.

"Want? Why should I want anything. I'm sure you want something. Some answers? Then let me give you them."

Parks leant back. "As you know we have an infestation problem. All the cities do. We knew it was a problem long ago, but how to deal with it? Then a young, naïve man came to me and old Precious with talk about a great Hunter. Problem solved. But what if we could sell the solution to other cities? I would be richer than Precious, rich enough to be mayor even of more than one city. So how to sell this wonderful product. Simple; get the fool to train you all up, then sell you on. Either expulsion or employment waits for each of you. Your choice. You were the first so you go back and tell them all. It would be best for all of you if you joined us."

Parks waved the guards, who thrust the bag over Piers's head, and led him out.

Chris waited in the open barred cell. Cold, and still wet, he felt pure rage. He had lost everything helping these people. Not only did he have the animal threat, he had a human one. Enemies all around, and now no way to fight back. Like a caged beast he was trapped and helpless.

"Boss," muttered Marty. "Sorry. Should never had said to come."

Chris shook his head. "Nobody tells me where to go but the winds, you know that. I chose, and chose badly. Now to get us out of here."

"You heard what Piers said," Marty whispered from the next cell. "They strip you, send you out at dusk with the aim you will die before morning."

Chris smiled, his old self. "Let them try to kill us. Just going outside at night? We live outside," he said.

Marty giggled. "No hammock this time, boss," he said.

"No hammock, but we sneak back in, steal our kit back, and save the guys. Then see them stop us."

"There is another way," said a new voice.

They looked towards it, and in a darkened corner of the jail Mayor Precious stepped into the light.

"Can you promise to stop these things?" he asked.

Chris saw the open honesty from the fat man, almost pleading.

"Yes," Chris said, keeping eye contact, searching.

"And stop Parks?" Precious looked around as if the agent could hear him.

"Parks? He's behind this?" Marty asked, jumping from his wooden bed.

"Yes. I found out earlier. He planned the whole thing from when Compton came to see me. He was there and must have played me from the start."

Chris shook his head. He had been so blind.

"How did Parks know we were out?" he asked the mayor.

"He had someone on the inside. Kept him informed," Precious said.

Marty and Chris shared looks. A mole, in their group?

Precious dropped a bundle on the floor, and a long rag wrapped pack, threw a metal key to Chris and left. Opening the cells they found their clothes in the bundle, and the pack held their rifles and some equipment they had taken from them. Now armed Chris found himself inside a nest of multiple types of enemies. Time to even the odds.

Chapter Ten

Precious walked quickly through the heavy rain to his office. He hated trying to move fast, but he had little choice. It was clear Parks was more of an enemy then he had though. He knew the office of mayor was always under threat, usually only kept because the person in the chair had first choice on new ventures. If someone had a sudden change in luck and money they could overtake. Or eliminate. Precious had worked hard, in his opinion, to be where he was. He owned a large portion of the factories, negotiated his way to high finance, and now earned quite a lot more than anyone else. That contentedness had let him grow soft. Parks had sneaked up behind him and now he was in trouble. He didn't know the man's plan but with Chris removed there was nothing stopping him. Now Precious had some small luck. He knew Chris was out there, Parks didn't. He smiled at the thought the power was returning to him. He didn't see in the rain the figure that was stalking him.

As he reached his chambers where he slept Precious checked the door for signs of movement, then entered. Crime was non existent in the city so locks were purely decorative. Inside his spacious rooms he had several pieces of furniture from the before time, and some his factories made. Quickly checking all the lower floor windows he felt satisfied and went to his bed chamber. The large, decorated wood bed was as he had left it. He changed to his night clothes and settled under the thin duvet. Within moments he was asleep, snoring loudly.

The cold wet hand over his mouth jerked him from a soft dream of wealth and pretty girls. The cold eyes under the wet hair made him flinch and try to scream. The hand held him tight. His unrealised fear Parks would try to eliminate him made his body tremble. The face still kept eyes locked to his, Precious felt the rain drip cold from the hair. Absently he worried his pillow would get wet. The heavy curtains were open, letting a dim glow in. Dawn. He had hardly slept. Still the eyes kept locked on him. As the light grew he saw familiar features. Fear gave way to confusion. Chris?

Chris saw the man calm and gently released his grip. Precious didn't move, but under the pale skin the red hand marks still remained. Stepping back Chris shouldered his rifle and motioned to Marty, who was hidden in the shadow of the window. It was still raining outside. In the growing dawn Precious saw damp patches on his carpet, and marks from their heavy boots. He frowned, about to complain when the noise of his side door opening froze the words in his throat. He knew the sound of that door, a gentle creak from the rain. He knew also it was being opened quietly. He looked imploringly at Chris, who smiled. The smile made Precious feel afraid, not for himself, but for the intruder. Precious saw a flash from the window, Marty had drawn a knife. Not a knife like Precious kept in his mayoral set for official functions, this was long, straight, with a serrated edge on the back blade, and a curve to the point. It winked with menace in the weak sunlight. Chris drew his, nodded to Marty to follow then slipped away.

Down the elegant staircase they ghosted along, staying close to the wall to minimise creaks from the floorboards. Below they heard the noise of untrained assassins trying to move with a stealth they never knew. Expecting their target to be asleep they bumbled around looking for the cellar door. Chris watched from the stairs, his clothing hiding him in the darkness. The plan of the would be killers slowly unravelled. They wanted to capture the mayor, knock him out, and drag his body to the cellar, then pretend he was attacked from below. They had heavy wooden clubs and a large metal mallet to incapacitate the mayor and make a hole in the cellar. Clever, Chris thought. But they had no idea. And they never would. Three men, against two. Chris smiled his evil smile again and slid to the floor.

Taking the stairs like an eel Chris slithered down to the floor, ignoring the pain in his chest from the edges of the steps and his equipment. With knife sheathed he crawled over the soft carpeting of the hallway and followed the three men. One of them paused, as if sensing something wrong. Chris noted the man and gave him credit for it. He wasn't as dumb as the rest. Still making too much noise the others finally forced open the stiff cellar door and vanished into the darkness. The third stayed back, with his club, as the other two went to make a hole. After some muttering and cursing the sound of metal on stone echoed up. Chris felt Marty touch his shin and moved aside so the younger man could move alongside.

The solitary man was too far to attack from their position. He was also too open to sneak up upon. Waiting while the others worked in the dark Chris planned his next move. He was still trying to sort details when the man unwittingly gave him a hand. Bored with waiting he started looking through drawers and cabinets in the hallway, and eventually, the nearest room. Slithering like a snake Chris followed, and peered around the bottom of the door frame to see a large table with chairs all around. Cabinets lined one side of the room, with huge windows on the other. Facing the morning sun the man was silhouetted by the yellow glow. The sun pierced the clouds, spearing the man in a searchlight. Chris wiggled under the table, hidden from the man, then knelt. Marty looked around the doorway, but was waved back. The man continued his search, pocketing some items he liked. Sensing his moment Chris sprang upwards, gripping the man's head in both arms, and twisting mid air. He aimed his leap to pull the man away from the cabinet. With only a creak the man's neck snapped and he fell limp to the floor, only one hand still in the drawer made a noise as it spilled some silver cutlery on the hardwood floor.

"What was that?" a voice called from below. The hammering had stopped, and Chris realised they had heard. He hurriedly pulled the body into a large cabinet, then slid back under the table. Steps rang from the cellar, and a man glanced into the dining room. Shaking his head at the mess he checked a pocket timer and called out quietly for the missing man, not using his name. His face showed only mild surprise as Marty pressed the knife against the man's ribs from behind, tapping him with the wooden club. With a sigh the second man fell to the floor. The third cursed politely and dropped his mallet, climbing the stairs. Without thinking he walked into the dining room, right into the muzzle of Marty's rifle. Chris sat on one of the guilt framed chairs, smiling. On the floor in front of him the two bodies lay. The third man paled, and tried to run, but the click of the safety catch stopped him. As the light grew Chris saw with shock the face of the man.

"Edgar?" he asked eventually.

The man hung his head in shame. Marty had frisked him for weapons, but beside his noisy timer he had only the mallet left down below. Chris stood, and with a closed fist struck the man formerly leader of one of his sections.

"Why, Edgar?" Chris asked. "Why? You had our trust, our support, our friendship."

Edgar kept his head down, but tears fell like gentle rain on the hardwood floor.

"Because I had no choice, boss," he murmured. "Parks had me. If I didn't do what he asked he would hurt my family in that torture chamber of his."

Chris leant forwards, glancing at Marty who never moved his rifles aim.

"Why didn't you say?" Chris asked. "We would have helped. We knew this was going to happen anyway. Me and Marty had a cache of gear for this eventuality."

Edgar shook his head and stayed silent.

"So what now, boss?" asked Marty.

Chris leant back, drew his knife and toyed with the blade. Edgar caught the reflection of the sun and watched as if hypnotised.

"We go ahead with the plan. This poor bugger will suffer if he don't kill the fat pudding upstairs, and his family too. He deserves it, but not them. Parks will pay for him."

"So?" said Marty, lowering his rifle.

"So, we get into Park's place, rescue anyone in there,

kill that evil bugger and leave. Then Eddie here can go back to being a dad, we can get our kit back, and finally flatten the nest."

"You got a plan?" Edgar spoke quietly, almost in reverence.

"Always have a plan, Eddie, you know that," Chris flexed his hand and stood. Sheathing the unbloodied blade he walked past Edgar and out to the hallway. There he met Precious trying to descend the stairs quietly.

"Chris?" he trembled as he spoke, clutching a metal bar in one hand and his robe around his prodigious waist in the other.

"All done, Mr Mayor. Just need to clean up some loose ends, remove a couple of threats, and then you can pay me."

Precious straightened to look more authoritarian. "We did not agree on a payment," he said.

"True," Chris smiled and walked past. Precious recoiled at the sight of Edgar, but Marty behind with his rifle on his shoulder made him relax. They left by the still open back door and vanished into the large designed garden.

Parks was starting to worry. His perfect plan that had so far gone exactly to schedule, had hit a roadblock in the shape of Chris and Marty. How they escaped he had no idea. The guard said nobody came or left, but Parks had him tortured to see if the man was saying the truth. He was, but that didn't help Parks, or the guard who died at Park's hand for failure. Now the two men were loose in the city somewhere. Nothing had come back from the men sent to remove the mayor, a nice accident to let Parks ascend to the white office. And now the black robed head of Internal Investigations was back in his lair he felt a little uncertain. There was no way Chris or Marty could penetrate his hive. The only way in or out was from the front door, thick wood and guarded front and rear. Should anyone try to escape they would be cut down with arrows from hidden wall slots. Should they survive that the floor traps would send their perforated bodies into a deep pit below to die slowly. Parks was safe.

A knock at his office door almost made him jump.

"Yes?" he demanded.

A nervous guard opened the door, bowed and tried to speak.

"Out with it, man," barked Parks.

"Sire, you wished a report from the alpha team?" the guard sweated in the cold glare of the man's eyes.

Wreathed with his demonic chair Parks seemed more terrible than any nightmare ever.

"Yes?" Parks snapped back.

"Sire, the tail you requested has lost them. They did not leave. Do you wish an interception team readying?"

"No, fool! Leave them be." Parks realised he sounded tense and forced himself to relax. The calm demeanour made the guard shake visibly. "Keep me updated, and add extra security on the front door, lookouts on the walls and get me something to drink."

The guard nodded, and bowed again. Parks waved him away and the relived man fled, making sure not to slam the door. Parks smiled to himself, and toyed with one of the faces on his chair. Maybe he should execute one of the captives he had, make the others weak and subservient? Thinking it over he decided his reputation was proof enough. The face he absently played with was getting old and brittle. Parks remembered the woman it had once belonged to. She tried to defy him, earning a space on the grisly chair.. She took a long time to die. Chris would take longer. Parks rose and throwing his robe around himself left to inspect his toys in the deep dark chamber below his office. His torture chamber. It had a date with a special guest.

"In there?" Chris asked with disbelief. Edgar nodded almost smugly. He had been asked by to show him the way to Parks, and surprised to have the big man's trust so soon he agreed with a word of warning. Now it seemed he was correct.

Chris looked over the building with a professional eye. It was deceptively simple, merely a wooden door, arched at the top, with two sleepy looking men guarding it with clubs. What you didn't see were the hidden hatches over the door, on the sheer smooth walls rising thirty feet over the stone alley, and the unseen eyes looking out. Parks had a clever set up. Hidden down a side street most would think this a small storehouse guarded for personal reasons by it's owner. They would never see the traps in store.

"No other way?" asked Marty, peering around the corner they hid behind.

"None," said Edgar. "The way he likes it."

Chris sat against a wall and thought. To get in would be hard, but to leave would mean his team would be at the mercy of Parks, and he had his kit to regain.

"Parks expects a frontal attack?" he asked eventually.

"Only way," said Edgar. "You can't get anywhere near. All that is on this level is a few guard areas, and a small office for the guard commander. Below is Park's office, captive holding area and a small kitchen. Under that is his torture chamber, and you don't want to go there." Edgar almost flinched at the thought. Chris smiled and closed his eyes. Edgar thought he was asleep, but Marty knew better. A plan was forming. After a few silent minutes Chris started snoring. Marty shook him.

"Don't disturb me when I'm planning, Marty. You know better than that," Chris said with a smile. He rolled to his feet away from the corner and stood. "Time to have some fun."

"Err, boss?" Edgar spoke softly.

"Yeah?"

"What about me?"

Chris smiled. "You, my son, get the best part."

Chapter Eleven

The sun was setting when Edgar Phipps stumbled to the door of Park's underground empire. Covered in blood and favouring his left leg he fell onto one of the guards, who finally recognised him through the blood on his face.

"What happened to you?" the guard asked.

"Take me to Parks," Edgar wheezed as if exhausted. The guard tried to help him stand, the other turning to open the door when two whistles sounded and the men fell like lead. None of the hatches opened, and Edgar after a brief check rolled his left trouser leg up and pulled out two smoke canisters. Pulling the pins he rolled one inside, and the other he left outside. Inside his jacket he pulled out a respirator. Two shapes emerged from the smoke in similar masks, weapons raised. Wordlessly Chris waved his silenced pistol at Edgar who led the way inside.

Once through the doors Chris quickly dispensed with the choking men inside. Marty climbed some steps on the side to clear the lookout hatches. Regrouping in the commanders office Edgar pointed out a door then pointed down. Chris nodded, stopping while Marty took a key from one of the dead guards and unlocked the door. Rolling a smoke canister down arrows flew from the walls. Chris couldn't see hatches. Must be holes angled to make it impossible to aim. Holstering his pistol he took the new rifle he had taken from the secret stash and checked the fat tube slung below the barrel. Marty mirrored him, then together they stepped from cover, aimed and fired. Two puffs of white smoke bloomed from the tubes, and the grenades hit the walls perfectly. Ducking back as they fired Chris and Marty missed the explosion, but the arrows stopped immediately, and as the dust mixed with smoke rolled past no more were fired.

"Any new holes, Marty?" Chris called.

"None but the ones I was born with," he called back. Chris knew Marty was enjoying himself. So was he if he cared to admit it.

"Best not get any new ones then, make a mess in here."

Marty laughed as he reloaded the launcher. "You too, makes it hard doing this alone, you help out sometimes."

"Cheeky git!" Chris laughed and threw the empty grenade shell from his launcher at Marty. Edgar watched in awe. Here they were attacking Park's fortress, and these two were joking around.

"You going first, boss?" Marty asked.

"Age before beauty, kiddo, and I'm both so I go first." Chris stood, looked through the clearing smoke and saw the thin walls were flattened by the blasts. He also saw cracks in the floor. Taking a large chunk of loose stone he threw it hard at the floor. It moved slightly. Satisfied Chris walking to the commanders office, returned with the chair from the desk, and threw it bodily into the shattered corridor. It bounced once then fell through the floor.

Holding onto the remains of the wall Chris shimmied

along until he could climb into the narrow space for the archers. Marty followed on the other side, both checking the bodies were dead. Edgar clumsily followed. Avoiding the next door they came through the archers doors, rifles raised ready. The small area was clear.

"Just had a thought, boss," said Marty pulling his mask off.

"What," asked Chris doing the same.

"These are as bit big for here," he said, patting the stock of his rifle.

"True," Chris said, examining his gun. "Pistol time again. Check and ready."

They shouldered their rifles and drew their pistols, stopping to reload the rounds fired at the front door. Moving slowly down the next corridor they checked every corner, every door, Chris leading, Marty at the back with Edgar in the middle. At one door Chris froze, then went inside. Edgar refused to go in, and Marty had to push him aside to get in. Before them was a large chair like a throne. Skulls and faces decorated it. Chris was looking closely at the faces, until one peeled off in his hands. Repulsed he dropped it and wiped his hands on his jacket. Real faces. Both stared in amazement at the grotesque display. Edgar stood behind them, tears on his face. He dropped to his knees and buried his head in his hands. Chris knew something was wrong, but Marty got there first.

"You ok?" he asked with an arm over the man's hitching shoulders. Slowly Edgar raised a trembling arm and pointed at the newest face pinned to the chair.

"My wife," he croaked, then dropped his head again. Chris looked at the face, the contortions of pain still on her face. Without the skull to give it shape it took the style of the carved skull it was pinned to. Without a word Chris dropped his pistol into its holster, took his rifle and cocked it. The sound made both men on the floor look up. They saw Chris, but not as they knew him. Even Marty felt fear, not of Parks, or his chair of horror. Chris looked evil, like the evil of the chair had possessed him. His face, once friendly, but firm now was locked into pure hatred, eyes burning, lips pressed so tight they were blue. Chris kicked the chair over, pushed past the desk, and left. Marty was unsure if he should follow, but Edgar was standing and red eyed followed, cocking his already loaded rifle, dropping an unspent round on the floor. Marty watched the brass casing bounce, then caught it, dropped it into his pocket and with a last look at the toppled chair he left.

Chris was already out of sight around a corner. The corridors curved like a wheel, stopping before they went full circle, then dropping down another flight to the next level. Edgar stopped by one door, and using a key from the guard area upstairs opened it. Inside was all of Chris' equipment. Taking his old rifle from a shelf Chris hugged it gently, then kissed the scuffed stock, putting his rifle back. The next door was an empty room. The third was larger. There were five guards inside, oblivious by their distance from the chaos upstairs. They were dropped quickly. All around on the floor were men, naked tied and gagged with sacks over their heads. Pulling the sacks off Marty recognised them as their team. Soon all were released, and clothed from the storeroom. Piers almost cried with joy.

Parks heard the noise upstairs, the soft bell rang from behind a small screen partition. With a sigh of regret he replaced the wicked curved blade to the velvet lined tray. Around him in the dark sub cellar was a selection of the most barbaric and horrific devices ever made, with only one purpose: the longevity of pain to the victim. Knives that could slice skin like paper, chains that could not be broken, whips, clips, and all manner or evil sharp items. Racks, metal boxes of spikes, hooks on the high ceiling and chairs with differing attachments were lined around the walls waiting another guest. Parks had found many secrets and unveiled a lot of plots from this room. If he was honest he enjoyed it. He had liked inflicting pain on people since he was a child. As an adult he learned you can manipulate others to hurt themselves. If all else failed he had his own temple of pain. Parks saw nothing wrong with that, the unfortunate women to cross his path did though. Many had perished here while Parks watched with sexual pleasure.

Crossing the polished wood floor Parks opened a small hatch in the heavy wood door. Echoing down the corridor from above he heard the voices carried clearly. The circular design was perfect, as Parks had intended. It channelled sound, while foiling attackers. He heard numerous voices he didn't know, but the agent had years of practice deciphering different voices from his myriad of hiding holes. One what Marty Fritz Herbert's, the other was the accursed Chris Spencer. Parks spat at the door and closed the hatch. The corridors led to the torture room, but not away. However, a man with his intelligence would never allow himself to be trapped like an animal. Dropping the thick metal bar into the slot on the door Parks had pretty much sealed himself in. With a last fond look around his toys he stroked an iron maiden softly, and then pressed a stone in the wall. The iron maiden slid forwards on its pedestal revealing a dark tunnel below. Parks dropped into the hole, then climbed back out, hurriedly collected the contents of the velvet-lined tray into a sack, and disappeared again.

Chris quickly inspected his troops. All were relatively unhurt from Park's capture, and aside from hunger they were keen to get back at him.

"Ok, Don? You take your guys and head for the

storehouse. Shuttle the kit and cars there. Pete? Take half yours to help them, the other to patrol the area. Keep an eye out for Parks, but don't do anything. If you see him send a runner and follow. Eddie and his gang are gonna tool up with us and prepare to hunt him down. Need some things first." Chris hefted his rifle and made show of loading it. He felt bad doing such a pantomime performance but the guys had been through a lot and needed the show of confidence.

Marty had finished his checks of the equipment; all was there. Satisfied Chris dismissed the men and smiled to Edgar. Without a word he turned away and headed down the corridor away from the exit. With Marty, Edgar and four others they went weapons raised down the narrow stone corridor curving right until it stopped abruptly at another set of steps leading down. Chris leading they descended the steps, curving back left into another corridor. Locked doors braced with metal lined both side. Checking them silently Chris saw nothing but empty cells, dark stains on the light stone floors. There was no light, no beds, and no toilet. Just a small square room made for those who were to die. At the end, there was only one door. Braced with thick steel bands corroded over time the door had marks on the front that Marty declared were from keys. As none had worked, Chris smiled and pulled a grenade from his belt.

"Universal key," he said and propped it against the hinges. Taking two more from Marty he waved everyone into the nearest cell, then pulled another grenade from his belt, yanked the pin and dropped it near the others. He slid into the cell as the blast rocked the foundations. Laughing he brushed the dust off his clothes.

"That helps wake you up," he smiled and took his rifle back from Marty. The door was on the floor inside the room, hinges bent and torn by the explosion. Moving carefully they inspected the room. Edgar and the four city men hesitated in fear. They knew the mystery of the room and feared it. Chris and Marty finished checking it, then stopped.

"What, guys?" Chris asked.

Edgar only shook his head. The others held back, not even looking in.

Marty slung his rifle. "We faced monsters, killers and the worst your man could throw at us. And we did it together," he said. "Come in and see."

Edgar still stayed put, the others watching him. Finally he spoke.

"It was in here that many died, for the pleasure of Parks. We knew of this room, but only as story. Mothers said to their children; 'it's the chamber for you' if they misbehaved. To see it, to know the truth, is hard. Too many vanished, too many suffered." He saw one of the racks of blades and shuddered. "We never had to face this."

Chris dropped his head and sat beside a rack.

"I know," he said quietly. "When I was younger I had a peaceful life. Wife, child, farm in a village. Comfy, quiet. We grew our food, sold some for tools, left alone. We saw convoys drive past and dreamed of living in the city. Clean streets, friendly people and safety. The village near us was hit by bandits, they killed everyone, including my brother who was there trading. We had no idea what had happened."

Edgar and the four city men came closer, oblivious to the rooms fear, trying to listen to a quiet Chris. Marty sat on a hard wooden chair covered in clamps. He had known Chris had a past, but never asked and he never told.

"Then one night it came. I had no idea what it was. It smashed our wall like paper. Once inside it ate. We couldn't get away. It ate everyone I knew, everyone I cared about. I was outside checking some crops when it came. I was trapped outside, and could do nothing but listen to the screams." A tear dropped from his face to the stained floor. Head down, voice a croak Chris spoke. "I made it to the other village, but it was empty, destroyed by bandits. Then I knew I was alone. I ran, and kept running, until I found my storehouse, full of weapons. Then I knew I didn't need to run." He stood, unashamed of the tears on his cheeks. "Now I don't run,

I don't stop, I don't give in. I found that bastard and blew it to hell, and ate it's flesh. I battered all the bandits I could find and kill whatever kills." He shouldered his rifle, and taking a large wooden beam began smashing the equipment. Racks, chairs, torture harnesses, all were smashed while Chris screamed in rage. Marty and the others fled the wildly swinging beam and huddled outside the broken doorway. Marty had never seen him like this, and found he was scared of Chris for the first time.

After everything was broken and bent, and his arms trembled, Chris dropped the beam. Panting and sweating he looked around him.

"Now it's Park's turn to face me." He kicked the iron maiden over, seeing the hatch underneath. Clipping his rifle to his belt, he drew a pistol and dropped into the hole. For a moment nobody moved, still in shock at the display of emotion. Chris' head popped up from the hole like a jack in the box. "Coming you lazy sods?" he called, then dropped back down. Marty shook his head and followed. Buoyed by the change in their leader and the speech he had given the rest followed.

Chapter Twelve

The tunnel was small and tight, but easily followed. Dust from years of neglect made them choke. Chris kept a fast pace, almost running, bent near double in the narrow space. He was well ahead by the time he reached the open space near the end. Marty caught up and saw they were in a large bell shaped chamber, strange stone walls without joins lined the walls, making the narrowing ceiling ending in another tunnel, this one heading straight up. A rusting ladder was fixed into the wall. Chris was checking the floor, seeing prints in the dust. They stopped at the ladder. Without a word Chris climbed up. Even in the near darkness he pushed on, small light being let in from above. After a near hundred-foot climb he stopped at the metal grate, and heaved it open. Light poured in, mid afternoon sun bounced from the walls, making the rainwater steam from the floor. Checking everyone had made it up Chris ducked into a nearby alley.

"Ok, I'm lost," he confessed. "No idea where we are. So from here we split. Eddie, you take your guys and make it back to the storehouse. Tell them to prep for a major assault on the nest. Me and Marty are gonna get Parks."

"What will you do with him?" Edgar asked.

"Don't know yet," said Chris, smiling. "See what I feel like."

Marty coughed. "Should we be after him solo, boss?" he asked. Chris shot him a pained look.

"Martin, you hurt me. How many nasty buggers have we taken out over the years? This guy is too smart and too well set up, but he's too confident. Won't take long." Chris waved the others away, but stayed in the alley. Once he was sure they were gone he leant against the wall. Suddenly he looked tired.

"Marty, I think I'm getting too old for this," he said quietly.

"Never," said Marty. "Plenty of meat left on the bone."

Chris smiled. "Maybe, but the bone is weary. Maybe I should retire."

"Retire?"

"Stop working, Marty. Never gave old Precious our price. A nice fancy house here, food, women. Can hang my gun on a wall and remind myself of the days in cold mud, rain, sun, dust and all the other nasty places we seem to end up."

Marty sat beside him, pulled a water bottle from his belt pouch and offered it over.

"Maybe, but you'll be bored," Marty said, taking the bottle back.

"True. But I am getting old. Only one mistake and you're gone. And I've been making loads."

"What mistakes?" Marty asked.

"Coming here, trying to train them, and trusting these people. We used to dream of living here when I was young. Now it's a nightmare, but I still want it."

"Maybe you do want it, but you don't need it. You need the free air, the open spaces, the real life." Marty closed his eyes against the sunlight and sighed. "I miss them. I wanted to come here more than you did, I made you come. Now we nearly got killed too many times, nearly lost everything and we still have a ton of enemies to face."

Chris sat up. "You're right, kiddo. It was always about the job. Time to do what we do best; do the job, get paid, move on."

Chris stood with a grunt and held out a hand.

"You coming? Time to kick some arse." Marty took the hand and stood beside his mentor. The age had dropped like a cloak. The old, quick, sharp Chris was back. Feeling the relief flood through him Marty smiled back and they headed out the alley.

In the mayors office Precious was absent. The Attendant made excuses but inwardly worried as to where the large man was. It was unheard of for Precious to miss a day in office, to be ill or detained. Unaccustomed to change the Attendant did as best he could but still struggled to work out what to do. Streams of visitors, each with their own little worries, poured through the doors and each needed to see the mayor urgently. The Attendant was running out of excuses. The joy he felt when Parks burst in outweighed the fear he usually felt about the agent. Politely he ushered him into the mayors office followed by complaints from waiting visitors.

"He is not here?" asked Parks once the doors were closed behind them.

"My apologies, Agent Parks, but the mayor had been missing all day. I was beginning to worry. I had hoped you might have some information on him. There is a tale going around his home was attacked last night."

Parks frowned at the flustered man. Without a word he turned away and left. The Attendant tried to close the doors to stop anyone seeing inside, barely shutting them in time. Parks pushed through the clamouring crowd, cape floating behind him.

Precious made a quick sandwich himself, his cook, cleaner and land keeper dismissed for safety. Taking the thick meal down to the dining room he paused at the still open drawers, flinched and headed to his bed chamber instead. Normally he never ate upstairs, but this was not normal times. The door banged downstairs as someone knocked. He'd had many visitors all day, and ignored them all. He was hiding, scared of Parks and his underworld agents. He had seen them outside, watching the house. Feeling confident he hadn't been seen Precious ate his large sandwich, meticulously keeping the crumbs from falling onto the bedclothes. After eating, he sat at the little desk in the corner and studied his ledgers. Business was looking up still, and some new legislation he had recently passed was making it look even better. The city was booming under his administration, the people richer, and the factories busier. Precious leant back in the chair, which groaned, and smiled. His little empire was strong.

A dark thought robbed his smile. His financial empire may be safe, but with nobody to work it, it would fall. They needed a leader, a ruler, fair and strong. Precious was that man, but not hiding in his bed. Standing abruptly, chair flying backwards, Precious washed in his large bathing room, selected his best mayoral robe and gown, laced his shining boots and left his room. He would stand strong in front of his people, show them he was in control, and he had their best interests in his heart. Face the peril, he though. Brushing past the agents outside he knew he was safe from any attack with the crowds in the street. They cheered his appearance, Precious actually blushed in pride. He raised his hands in acknowledgement, and walked to his offices. The crowd followed, still cheering, while agents tailed from a distance.

The Attendant nearly collapsed when Precious walked through the waiting area, ignored everyone, and let himself into his office. Once behind his massive desk he felt right, the captain of a ship sailing stormy seas. He was on his bridge where he should be. Calling on the tube he summoned his first visitor.

Chapter Thirteen

Chris and Marty walked the streets with an air of men who had nothing to do. Marty even tried chatting up some of the local young ladies, their skimpy summer outfits arousing his interest. After Marty got his fifth address, Chris made a low grunt, barely audible. Neither dropped the impression, but they lowered their voices.

"Wassup, boss?" Marty asked.

"Tail. Got two behind. One in white like that tart you just chased, the other in grey." Chris smiled and then roared with laughter as if Marty had told a brilliant joke. Marty laughed too, and bowed sarcastically as Chris offered him a chair at an open-air café. They pretended to read the menus while they chatted, not looking anywhere, or appearing alert. Their rifles were propped against the table.

"Seen them," Marty said, then waved over a waitress.

"I know. You must work on your observations," Chris said, taking another look at the menu. They ordered water, then Marty asked for the toilet.

"Out the back, sir," the nervous waitress said, eyeing their weapons. In the land of white gauze and soft shoes, they looked as well placed as a diamond in a goat's ass.

Marty thanked her, and stood, stretched, then followed her inside. Chris stuck out his booted feet, yawned, and sipped the water. He heard the two sets of soft shod feet move closer, and to improve the act dropped his hands to his lap, lowered his head, and looked like he had fallen asleep in the sun. The soft swish of metal on cloth came from behind, the soft-soled shoes whispering on the stone walkway. Chris timed it perfectly.

As the knife flashed to slice his throat Chris rolled to

one side, raised the pistol he had hidden in his lap and fired. The knife was ripped from the hand of the man in grey, sent spiralling into the road flashing sunlight. Firing again Chris hit the man in his left leg, dropping him. The man in white held his knife by the handle, but reversed it ready to throw. A shot from the café hit his shoulder, making him drop the knife and hold the wound. Marty came from the café, pistol raised. Chris kicked the knives away and dragged the grey man to join his accomplice. Kneeling close to his face Chris grabbed the grey tunic and looked into the man's eyes.

"Parks?" he asked. The man stared back silent. Chris gave him some credit for holding the stare, but held his until the man cracked. "Parks?" he repeated. Still the man stayed silent. Chris dropped the man, and pulled back the bolt of his rifle. At the click both men looked at the scuffed muzzle.

Marty kept his pistol on them. He kicked the grey man in his wounded leg, making him cry out.

"You want another, sunshine," Marty asked, and kicked him again. The man gave him the dirtiest look Marty had ever seen and spat at them. The café customers crowded around the scene and muttered their disgust at such behaviour.

Chris aimed his rifle at the white dressed man. "Only need one to talk to," he said and pulled the trigger. The rifle clicked. It was empty. Chris saw with satisfaction the damp patch growing on the white short leg trousers. This made the crowd mutter more. Taking the man by his leg Chris dragged him away, Marty following with the grey man.

In a nearby alley they found nothing, so left the men. Marty still broke their legs to stop them following. Chris frowned.

"Bit much, ain't it?" he said as they walked the hot road to the mayor's offices.

"Nah," said Marty. "Something to remember us by. When it rains they will think of us."

Chris laughed and upped the pace. The sun was starting to wane, evening wouldn't be far and they had much to do. Finding familiar ground they headed for the mayor, then turned away to the storehouse. Inside there was a frenzy of activity. Sentries covered the roof, front entrance and the nearby area. Patrols came and went. Inside equipment was sorted and arranged. Chris and Marty accepted the greetings from his men, and went halfway up the steps. Stopping Chris held out his hands like Precious, waiting for the noise to die down.

"Ok, chaps, this is it. I found the nest with the last patrol and it is massive. No idea how we will take it out but we will. Get some sleep, rotate patrols like normal and be on your toes. Parks is still out there some place, and I want him. But first we do the job. Fun later."

The men laughed and cheered him. Chris waited for the noise to abate again.

"I'm getting my head down too, so shut up." They laughed at this, making Chris wait again. "First light we move out. Be ready, now sod off." He turned his back on their laughter and dropped into his hammock. Wondering how long it had been since he last slept Chris dozed off.

Downstairs Piers was organising the men. With Chris and Marty absent he had taken command unofficially. The men liked him, and they wanted to make him proud. Being the first 'recruit' he held status over them, like the first chosen. Marty leant on a window frame in the office where Chris was already snoring, and watched the officer organising the men below. His eyes were aching and felt like they had been dried in an oven. He climbed into his own hammock, wriggled into a comfy position and slept, ladies in white gauze dancing in his dreams.

Chapter Fourteen

Parks was in trouble. Once Chris and Marty invaded his lair he knew it was over. All his money, all his careful planning had gone terribly wrong. He owed a lot of influential people money, and most wouldn't wait.

Crime was unknown in the city, but loan sharks still had teeth. He had plenty saved up, hidden in a secret place near the west gate. Gold, the international coin, and some gems. It was to there he fled. He had to leave the city, something he regretted. He had business here, but that would be reclaimed by his creditors, liquidised and distributed. His home, his staff, even his family would be made property of those he owed. He made a gamble, and the bigger the stake the bigger the reward. This time it hadn't paid off. No matter. With his money in his possession, and carte blanch to leave on any convoy he chose he could start to influence another city. They didn't care what someone had done elsewhere, as long as they paid to them. He'd start again with a new city and work his way in again.

Checking the convoy lists for outgoing trucks he found one was leaving for another city that evening. Unusual for one to go at night, but maybe a special Parks thought. Quickly he went to his stash, pulled a suede sack from a loose stone in a wall, and tested the weight. Felt right, about 60 kilos or so. Leaving the stone out he walked to the convoy area. He slowly became aware of the group of unsavoury looking men following him. Quickening his step, he almost jogged to the convoy door. Seeing the notice board next to the entrance he almost ran, but instead stopped dead. Beside the notice two very familiar faces waited.

"Nice to see you again Richie," said the taller of the

two. Dressed in black, as was his associate, the man was one of the big sharks, Casper. The other, shorter and less friendly looking was Alfie, who was rumoured to have loaned to half the city, and caused more broken bones due to late payments. Parks had promised them a fortune, with the plan to pay them when Precious was toppled. Now they expected payment. Parks knew he had to bluff.

"Hey, Casper," he smiled as best he could. "Nice to see you too." Alfie grunted.

"Seems Alfie and me agree," said Casper. "Looks like you are skipping town. Next convoy looks good." Casper pulled the schedule from the board, revealing another underneath. Parks knew he'd been tricked. He had the list of convoys on his desk, as they all knew.

Alfie grunted again, unfolding his tree trunk arms. He had no weapons, but needed none either. Parks paled slightly, his cool failing.

"So, Richie, why are you here?" Casper asked.

"I, err, was going to expand," Parks clung to the weak lie like a lifebelt. "Time to broaden the horizons, conquer new markets, control new investments."

"And the bag?" Casper nodded to the sack.

"Just knick knacks, Casper. Creature comforts."

Alfie grunted.

"Agreed, old friend," said Casper with false realisation. "Very good point. Seems young Ritchie here had some bother earlier. Lost his little play pen, and his place on the board of influence. Means he has no money now, and not looking at the list properly means only one thing."

The group of men following had closed the net around Parks, trapping him, Alfie and Casper like kids on a playground fight. Sensing it was going badly Parks cracked, dropping the sack and pulling a pistol from his belt. Holding it in a shaking hand at Casper he snarled in hollow defiance.

"Took you long enough, spook. Thought you and the man tree were clever? I played you as a cat does with a mouse. Now unless you want that silly face of yours all over the wall move aside and let me go. I may even send you some money later, when I am done laughing."

Casper looked hurt. Alfie just grunted. Parks still held the pistol, shaking so hard it wavered between the two sharks.

"A crying shame, eh Alfie?" Casper sighed, tutting. Alfie grunted.

Parks looked near hysteria. "I'll do it!" he shrieked. "I'll kill you dead."

"Shame," tutted Casper. "Such potential. Sorry to do this Ritchie but business is business. You know how it is. You have your little play pen, I have mine. Yours is gone, smashed from what I hear. Mine is still very much intact. Let me show it to you." With a flick of the eyes, one man took the pistol from a shaking Parks, and another put a sack over his head. Pushed to the ground the sack was kicked until it stopped moving, and then dragged away like a sack of refuse. Casper opened Park's bag, smiling at the gold inside.

"Like I said, a shame. Still, pay day for us old boy," he said. They watched the now still sack being dragged away, then got into the back of their chauffeured buggy, Casper still searching the bag "Hello!" he said with surprise. "Nice little toy he gave us. A gift no less, old friend. We must use it the way he wished it, to show our appreciation of course." Casper flourished the velvet liner filled with Park's favourite tools of torture. Alfie grunted.

Chris woke with a start, almost falling from his hammock. He shouted a whoop of joy, making Marty jump, roll over and fall with an oomph from his hammock on the dusty floor.

"Wha'?" Marty asked, rubbing his head. "Wassup?"

"Got it!" Chris shouted, dancing with joy.

"Looks incurable," Marty moaned, sitting on the floor still. Chris danced a little jig, then bolted through the door. Wondering if he had finally cracked Marty shrugged and tried to get back into his hammock. Chris rushed back in, pushed him out again.

"No time lazy bugger! Dressed and to work, to work!" he ran out again.

Grumbling under his breath Marty wiped the sleep from his eyes and pulled on his trousers. With no windows or timepiece he had no idea how long he had slept, but it didn't feel long. Downstairs Chris was already rushing around shouting orders. Boxes were moved, the marker wall cleaned and Chris lined them up in front as if he was giving a lecture. When Marty staggered down the stairs Chris was drawing on the wall with a grease pen.

"So?" Marty yawned.

"Plan, kids," Chris said, dropping the pen and rubbing his hands together. He looked charged, ready to explode. He had a plan, Marty realised, an amazing plan only Chris could pull off. Seems like the job was coming to an end. The silence as everyone looked in expectancy at Chris was solid, only the hiss of rain outside like static broke the silence.

Pointing to the drawing, a large squashed semicircle Chris spoke. "So the nest is in a giant cavern like this.

There are hundred of the things, like a plague down there. Loads of nasties and not enough of us. We'd need an army, and more guns then we have. Even then, one attack wouldn't do it, they would run. We need one big blast to wipe them out, and I have nothing that big, that won't destroy the cavern too. Can't make big holes in the ground!" Chris giggled gently, still rubbing his hands. He stooped and picked up the pen.

"So we use something else," he said. "There is water pouring in here," he marked an 'x' about halfway up the left hand side of the semicircle. "I think that's the river. It's in the right place. We blow that, water floods them out. We clean out the tunnels. Job done." with a flourish he coloured in the semicircle.

"Err, boss?" asked Piers, sat at the front.

"Yes, son?"

"Err, how do you plan to blow that? Explosives need setting and if it's on the other side we can't throw it."

Chris smiled like a teacher explaining a simple premise to a slow child. "We simply us a mobile explosive."

"Rocket?" Piers asked.

"Rocket," Chris replied. "From the small cave in wall where me and Marty first observed the nest we can aim two rocket launchers at the wall. The trick is getting out before we get washed away too. It's too far to run, too far to have a rope, and if the tunnel in floods we can't tie ourselves in."

"Suicide mission?" one of Edgar's men, called Alex asked.

"Not really, Al," Chris said. There is one way. We set them to go on a timer. The launchers use electronic triggers to fire, squeeze it, and a signal is sent to fire. Saves accidents and mechanical components to fail. We aim them, set a timer, and leave. That's the trick. We need two mounts capable of taking the recoil, a timer and we need it down there. Some of you were metal smiths, Derek, Terry, Bob? You make the mount. You know the recoil and how to make them strong enough. I want a team to scout the nest, Eddie; you take five, go like ghosts. I'll make the timers and modify the launchers. The rest of you keep your eyes peeled. The tunnels around the nest will be filled with running dinosaurs, and they won't be hungry, so spread out amongst them and be ready. Attack tomorrow noon, when they should be mostly asleep. This is it, people. Let's do what we came here to do." With a wave he dismissed them.

As the group broke up Piers hovered over towards Marty.

"Err, Marty?"

"Yo, Piers," Marty gave him a pat on the shoulder, infected with Chris' enthusiasm.

"I was thinking, when this is over, I'll be back to my old job," Piers said.

"It will never be over," Marty said. "They are getting in from the outside somewhere, and all this meat in one place? Tempting choice. There will always be a job here."

"True," Piers brightened. "I was hoping, though, to leave the city, when you do. Ride shotgun as you say."

Marty looked deep and long at Piers. He saw no joke, no gag, just serious hope. He knew the little officer was bored of his tedious job, but to leave the luxury of the city? Even Marty was struggling to come to terms with leaving, and he'd been there only the summer. The rains were coming, time to collect their meat curing in the stashes, and bed down in the bunker before the snows came. Leave the city with its clean streets, food, women, clean water, women, safety and women?

"Piers, I think your place is here, but as head of these guys. You ain't a Hunter, but you are a bloody good Officer of the Law, and you shall be one. Outside is great, but you're an insider. Stay on the inside." Marty put his hands on Piers's shoulders. "Keep a warm space for us, we won't be leaving forever."

Piers smiled. "And a warm filly for you?"

"Or two," Marty laughed, and with an arm over Piers's shoulder they walked to the weapons racks to clean and prep their rifles.

The sack was pulled off. Bright light made Parks' eyes water. Slowly his eyes adjusted and shapes formed, one tall and thin, the other short and stocky. The taller one held up something to the light. As his eyes focused Parks saw it was one of his knives. Casper examined it closely.

"A fine piece of workmanship if ever I saw one," Casper said. Alfie grunted. "See the curved back edge? Means it will cut cleanly, but should you push it straight in, it won't stick, and that little groove in the blade releases the suction of the flesh. Very nice equipment, Ritchie, very nice." Casper waved the small blade in front of his face, letting the light flicker. Parks sat motionless, his blood already draining from his face in fear. Alfie watched with barely the trace of a smile on his face.

Casper stood and sat on the edge of a low table beside Parks. On it the sack of gold, and the velvet wrap were laid out, the tools already lined up neatly. Casper replaced the one he had taken from a gap in the centre. Taking up one from the front the smiled at Parks.

"They say you can learn a lot from a man by the tools he uses. I think we should learn some more of our old friend, Ritchie, agreed Alfie?"

Alfie grunted. Parks screamed.

Chapter Fifteen

Oblivious to the fate of his next target Chris pushed the men hard, making sure they were ready. He knew the risks involved, the chance for failure. Removing the nest with as many of the animals killed in the flood would make the clean up of the tunnels easier. Small patrols could finish the job where a large force would be needed if they let too many escape. To stop this he mapped the tunnels leading to the nest and mined them. He also posted men armed with grenades, mines and remote explosives at all the exits. Once he was satisfied he took Marty, Piers and a small detachment to the entrance they had first discovered the nest from. The forlorn stone archway looked worse after the downpour had washed most of the smaller shards of stone away, leaving just cleaned chunks scattered on the small steps leading from the surface. The opening still gaped like a mutated mouth, cracked stone for teeth. Chris felt the gentle breeze from the murk, the smell of rotten meat and decay on it. Licking his lips he gave a weak smile, then nodded silently to Piers, who nodded back nervously, clutching his rifle. Behind him four men, unarmed, got a better grip on the launchers. Marty was already pressed against the wall to the side of the hole, searching the dark for movement and sounds.

With a moments hesitation Chris sighed and ducked into the tunnel. The small space at the top of the long steps down was still deserted, stone littering the smooth floor, debris from the large dinosaur breaking through a wall still carpeted the floor. Without moving the larger pieces and making no noise they ghosted along, pausing frequently, listening. Sweat poured down their faces as the small knot in their guts grew. Fear set in, but Chris noted with pride none of them let it show, or turned back. Heading down the long stairs against the wall Chris noted the light was brighter down here. The rains had cleared the grates in the ceiling, letting more light in. something else was wrong, so wrong it made him pause. Marty, at the back, sensed the change and crept beside Chris.

"Wassup?" he breathed into Chris' ear.

"Don't know," he replied, softly as the wind. It was so quiet he could hear his heart pound in his ears.

The men shuffled nervously behind. Their job was simply to follow to the drop point, unload the launchers, then leave. They didn't like the wait. Chris flashed them an angry look for making noise, then realisation dawned, draining the colour from his face. Around them eyes opened, glowing in the small light. An ambush.

Without moving Chris let out a soft moan, and for the first time felt lost. He had no idea what to do. Faced in this unknown territory, unlike his usual terrain he had relied on memory and experience. But these animals lived in a city, not the plains. They lived differently, and hunted differently. Panic rose, making him feel sick. Sweat dripped his face. Marty saw him shake and the panic was transferred. The eyes slowly moved closer. They knew their prey was there, immobile and inoffensive. An easy kill.

Flashes blinded everyone, making man and dinosaur alike wince and turn away. The ear shattering report of a rifle bounced off the curved walls, making everyone shout and cover their ears. Explosions rocked the air, blasts rustling hair and blowing clothes. Chris looked up against the flashes to see Piers had stood to face the animals and opened fire, pausing long enough to flip two grenades. With shame and rage Chris rose and fired his rifle. The sudden attack had spooked the animals, but they were not beaten. The four unarmed men huddled behind as Chris and Piers, joined by Marty, kept up constant fire into the mass of bodies. Relief came from above as the reserve team, hearing the shooting, came down the long stairs and joined in, adding ten rifles to the mix. Unable to withstand the hail of bullets the animals ran. Chris, fumbling with another magazine ran after them screaming. Marty ran too, trying to stop Chris. Piers shouted for half to stay put, the rocket carriers and the other five to join him. Together, covering each other like on patrol the headed down the raised platform and into the dark tunnel after Chris and Marty.

Piers burst from the dark tubular tunnel into a large open space, easily big enough to swallow the storehouse several times over. Just as Chris had said water leaked in a small fall from the far wall. Mounds with broken egg shells were dotted around the floor, and the smell of rotten meat made him gag. But of dinosaurs the space was empty. Chris stood, rifle in one hand and stared. Marty put a hand on his shoulder.

"Well," said Chris eventually, "that makes the job harder." The nest was abandoned.

Back at the storehouse Marty had signalled everyone to regroup and plan the next move. The nest had been long abandoned, clearly after the big animals attack, and the evident infiltration of Chris and Marty had made them leave for safer living. How they would find them, Marty didn't know. All he knew was they had to find them somehow. The death toll had reached the two hundred mark, and now people were being killed in broad daylight, even in crowded areas.

An inspection of the animals that had attacked them showed they were malnourished, tired and dehydrated, most likely from their long wait to ambush any returning attackers, or early warning from larger predators. Damage in the nest area showed the larger animal had broken in, then followed another tunnel to attack Chris and Marty. And if that one was down there, more could be. Feeling underpowered and under prepared Marty didn't like the odd. He also didn't like the change in Chris. The man was visibly shaken, once he had emptied his rifle into the ambushing dinos and his mad dash into the nest site he seemed drained, empty, listless. He had to be led to the car, driven back, and now sat alone on the roof, lost in himself. Usually he'd be cleaning his rifle, reloading the used magazines and getting ready. Instead he had lost all interest in everything. Marty had cleaned the rifle, almost reverently, and reloaded the dented black magazines with dull copper rounds.

Stepping onto the roof, feeling the cool breeze of evening on his tired face Marty nodded to the sentries on the edges, then looked to Chris. His mentor was sat on the edge, feet dangling, head down. He looked almost as if he were asleep. Making sure he made a lot of noise Marty made a brief inspection of the rooftop, then sat near Chris, who still didn't move.

"Getting colder," Marty said gently. Chris was silent. "Must be the snows coming soon."

Chris still stared at the river, fuller now from the rain, as it flowed steadily past. Small things floated in it. Bits of wood, paper, the odd dead bird. Not many birds survived now. For some reason they didn't live well in these times. Chris kept silent, and Marty leaned forwards to see his face. No tears, but a horrible emptiness in his eyes. Once bright and clear they were glazed like a corpse. If it wasn't for the slow rising of his shoulders Marty may have thought him dead.

"Yep, deffo getting chilly," Marty tried again. He rubbed his hands theatrically to imitate warming them.

"Marty?" Chris said finally.

"Yes, boss?" he replied.

"Bugger off."

Never had Chris told Marty to leave in that tone. It spoke as an order. There was no negotiation, no room for discussion. It was a dismissal and a command. Marty paused, unable to react. He felt hurt, for the first time he could remember. Chris had always been there for him, since being found lost and confused, not even knowing his real name Chris had taken him under his wing and carried him. If he needed support it was there, a down day? Chris lifted him up. He was father and brother to him. He had always been the one to make everything seem better, no matter how bleak. When Marty told Chris to leave, Chris did, but came back with a joke and a laugh. Marty realised that was what Chris needed. It was his turn to lift Chris up.

Standing he turned to walk away.

"You need to work on your walking, noisy bugger," Chris said.

Half turning back Marty smiled. "Thought it didn't matter, you deaf old git."

"Less of the old or I'll pitch you into the river. Time you learnt to swim."

"You couldn't pitch a stone. Old weak man, see you throw anything other than your food."

"You'll sharp see how far I throw when you're up to your neck in river," Chris said, turning and leaping like a cat, taking Marty at the waist and rolling them both over. As they play fought on the flat roof the sentries looked in horror, until the laughs and soft punches calmed their fears. After a few minutes they broke apart, panting.

"You still can't fight," Chris said with a grin.

"Beat your ass, granddad," Marty shot back.

"Never, I just got bored. Not worth the effort." Chris stood, and held out a hand to Marty. The younger man paused, looking at the dirty palm, then took it and stood.

"So what's the plan, boss?" he asked.

Chris studied the river again. "Seriously? I have no idea. Out there I would just hunt them down, track the new nest and destroy it." he waved at the walls, obscured by the buildings over the river.

"I think we are out of our zone here," Marty said.

"You're right," Chris smiled. "We need an expert." Grabbing Marty's arm he led him to the stairs. "And the snows are weeks off you soft bugger."

Half way down the steps Chris shouted for Piers.

"Yeah, sir?" Piers called back.

"You and Eddie get over here."

With Edgar and Piers leaning over a crude map of the city on a large roll of paper placed on a metal box Chris pointed with his knife.

"The original nest was here," he pointed to the entrance near the main bridge. "They legged it from there, but there's a lot of them, so where? You guys used these tunnels before to get to work. We need a space bigger then that one, nearby and easily defended."

Edgar leaned closer to the map. "I didn't go that way, boss, but Frederick did. Hey, Freddie?"

Frederick Pointer came running over, almost sliding

into the box. "Yessir?"

"Where near that nest site is similar in size?" asked Edgar.

Freddie studied the map, tracing the untidy lines with a shaking finger. With his tongue out his mouth he almost muttered to himself.

"Here, sir," he said finally, stabbing his finger on a place near the original nest site.

"Good," said Chris. "So we go there and wipe them out. How many tunnels lead there?"

"All of them," said Freddie.

"Nuts," said Marty.

"Maybe not," said Chris. "If we could flush them out, maybe thin the numbers. If we patrol the tunnels, stopping anything we find, we can condense them into their nest. They have to protect that."

"How?" asked Piers. "They are not easy to kill. Most of those we got in the tunnel were weak and tired, and they still took a lot of killing."

"The point exactly, kiddo; we killed them." He slapped Piers on the back so hard the man went sprawling over the map. Impatiently he waited for Piers to move, the straightened the map. "Look here, we go in small they will have a tasty snack. We go in as a large force we may find nothing, we may hit pay. Either way we can finally start evening the odds, and make them fear us. We have the fire power, we have the manpower. Let's go kick their stiff tailed arses."

Marty saw the old Chris coming back, bouncing from defeat to attack. He felt the enthusiasm of the hunt, but also fear. What if Chris froze up again?

"Eddie? You and Freddie make a more detailed map of the area. I need to cover that wall over there, with something to symbolise groups so we know where they are headed. Piers, you get the fun job of leading them with Pete and half of Don's group. The rest patrol, or sleep. I'm off to see Tubs about more food. Getting hungry and bored of this crap." Stabbing his knife into the metal box through the map Chris turned, walked out the storehouse and up the hill. Marty and Piers exchanged looks, then went to their tasks.

Chapter Sixteen

The Attendant gave Chris his customary apologetic look as he waited for the mayor. After all he had done Chris felt he was owed, old Precious was alive purely because of Chris and Marty. The wait was expected, others had crowded the small waiting space with backlogged concerns. With his scuffed boots stretched out Chris settled into the comfy chair and waited. The man next to him on his left made an unimpressed grunt and tried to shuffle away. The man to his right coughed, then spoke when Chris looked at him.

"Mr Spencer, I presume?" The man spoke softly, and held out a thin hand.

"Yep," said Chris, gingerly taking the hand, then winced at the vice like grip.

"Donaldson, I run a few little places down the waterside, your storehouse included. I know our excellent mayor is financing your enterprise, however I would like to highlight my worries over the condition of my premises." Donaldson was polite in his speech, but Chris felt the distaste hidden in the friendly words.

"Rest assured, Mr Donaldson, that your 'premises' are in safe hands, and shall be returned to you once this is over in far better condition then when I took residence there," Chris said, in his best voice. Donaldson frowned, trying to work out if he was being insulted. Satisfied with the response he nodded cordially and stood.

"I feel my business can wait, the mayor is very busy, as am I. Good day, Mr Spencer." He nodded to Chris again.

"Mr Donaldson," Chris nodded back crisply. Donaldson hesitated, then nodded to the Attendant and left. With the hint of a smile the Attendant left his desk and gestured for Chris to see the mayor.

Precious was sat still in his finest robes behind the large dark wood desk. Mounds of paper hid most of his bulk leaving a flustered round face looking through a gap made in the center.

"Ah, it's you. Yes?" Precious spoke almost as condescendingly as Donaldson. Chris was taken aback by his abrupt tone.

"Just asking for more food rations," Chris said.

"You ask for what?" Precious said, grated by the fact Chris didn't use his title.

"More food. They guys are pulling double patrols and what we have was barely sufficient."

Precious looked as if Chris had asked for the city.

"Mr Spencer, we have neither the provisions, nor the facilities to provide food for your party. We have been more than generous so far, and to ask for more is almost insulting. You have been here far longer that you predicted, and have failed in your task. I suggest you complete what you set out to do, then the problem of supplies is removed. Good day."

Precious selected a piece of paper and began writing. Chris stared at the round head bent intently on his work. Rage boiled like a fire, making him red. He leapt forwards, scattering papers and seized Precious by his ornate robes.

"Now listen to me you fat prick. I saved your life from your own stupidity. I saved your ass from your own people, and I saved your position on that chair from your own incompetence. Now you get me what I ask for, or fight your own battles."

Precious quivered under the strong grip. Stuttering he tried to speak until Chris slapped him hard.

"I, I will see what I can do," Precious managed eventually, the red mark from Chris' hand glowing on his pale cheek.

"Good. I appreciate that. Good day, sir." Without waiting Chris left the mayor to pick up his disturbed paperwork still shaking.

Outside the Attendant, having heard the conversation through the tube, gently led Chris to one side.

"I am impressed, Mr Spencer, that you have lasted this long."

"Excuse me?" Chris replied.

"Let me explain." the Attendant sighed, and checked

nobody else was looking. "This is a different world to the one you used to know. Here the words are soft, but stronger. A meaning is made not from actions, but from how you speak. Great power is shared and controlled by those who do nothing physical, but move in circles higher than ours. You must speak to them like they speak to each other, to integrate yourself, or risk being ignored like an irritating child."

"Why are you telling me this?"

The Attendant smiled. "We outsiders need to stick together," he said, and returned to his desk.

Chapter Seventeen

The tunnel was dark and cold, a chill breeze drifted through almost lazily, like it wasn't bothered. Dust swirled in the gloom in small curls. The paths were deserted now, too dangerous for anyone to walk the darkened tubular route. The metal rails in the centre were covered in a sprinkling of dust. The smell on the breeze was rancid, of death. Rotten meat, faeces and decay rode the wind. Piers made a face as he paused, sweat dripping and leaving small craters in the dust. Behind him nine of his best were half crouched, covering their arcs, making sure the ten man snake had eyes all around. Piers knew this area, he used to walk it to his patrol area. The grates in the ceiling had been cleaned from above by a lucky few who got to avoid patrol duties. Down here, there was no support, no escape, no place to hide.

The tunnel was a huge curved half pipe that arched over ten feet above them. Lined with grey moulded stone of some kind there were electric lights, but they had never worked in all the time Piers had used the route. The lighting from grates above and flaming torches laid by thoughtful residents was what used to guide the way. Now the holders were dark and the grates clogged. To his right Piers saw alcoves along the wall, and a ledge narrower than hid foot half way up the wall. He often imagined some giant worm making this tube, the rolls of cabling lining the wall above the ledge like slime from a snail, or silk from some giant spider.

Ignoring the sudden irrational fear of giant worms Piers forced his mind back to the job. There were spoors on the ground, but they were old and dry, giving little scent. From what he had learnt from Chris that meant this way had been left alone for some time. The strange footprints were faded from dust and water that dripped from the grates above, or ran from the walls in small streams where it had found a hole in the man made stone. The constant drips echoed off the acoustically sound walls and made any noise seem much louder. Piers had to make himself hold back when anyone made a noise behind. He half turned and looked at his number two, a sane and sensible man called Monty Dirks. With his face blackened by the dust and sweat, and under the thick gloom only his eyes showed clearly, brilliant white with black pupils. He gave Piers a smile, still keeping his rifle over his arc.

"We good, mate?" he asked.

Piers nodded. "So far." They kept their voices hushed. "Seems to have been empty for a while. I get nothing on the wind."

Monty smiled a relieved smile. Over the past month since their rescue from Parks he and the men had gained a new found respect for Piers, who had become a third leader alongside Marty and Chris.

"Where next then?" asked Alvin Peterson, the youngest of the group and the victim of many of the jokes.

"We head on to the next opening, then wait for Eddie's group from the north," said Piers. "Keep your eyes open, ears tuned and fingers off those triggers. No need to make it too obvious we are here."

The men smiled, white teeth glowing in dark faces. Maintaining their arcs they moved on. At a half crouch they walked swinging their rifles through slow curves, each facing the opposite of the one in front so they looked from above like a ten legged insect. Although up against the left hand side of the tunnel they still kept their rifles aimed out in case an alcove or sudden opening contained any surprises.

Piers led, grim faced. He knew that at the from the front he was the most vulnerable. Chris insisted they took it in turns to lead, but Piers wanted only to take the front, to prove his courage, and to lead by example. With his rifle ahead of him, finger sweating on the trigger he looked down the sights into the gloom. His heart beat a fast tempo in his ears, requiring him to take deep breaths to clear them. His mouth was dry and sticky, but he didn't drink. After all his patrols he ended up exhausted and dehydrated, but he didn't care. He had never lost a man.

Ahead the walls became more defined, and to their right it opened up into a small space only double the width of the tunnel. The floor was three feet higher, and the walls were tiled white. He felt a twinge of embarrassment when he saw Edgar's group was already there waiting.

"Thought you got lost," said Edgar, leaning on the curved edge of the tunnel.

"Nah," said Piers accepting a hand up onto the platform. "Just doing the job properly."

Edgar laughed. "Still here, ain't I?"

"Just."

"That's good enough for me," joked Edgar, leaning back against the wall. With his men covering both ends of the tunnel Edgar watched as Piers's team vaulted the ledge up to the platform. They joined the others covering the dark holes.

"Keep looking for anything unpleasant," said Monty.

"Like your feet?" asked Alvin.

"Like my boot up your behind."

"How about you go in, Al, and see where they are?" suggested Piers.

"Nah," said Alvin. "You know me, get lonely by myself, why I joined you bunch or inbreeds."

"Inbred?" asked Edgar.

"Inbred," repeated Alvin.

Monty kept his rifle aimed into the darkness, but knelt down to reach into his pocket with his left hand. Pulling out a dead mouse he had found he flicked it to Alvin, who screamed childishly when it hit the side of his face. Falling from the platform he rolled on the dust before regaining his composure.

"Very funny!" he complained, brushing the dust off his jacket.

"Keep looking for anything unpleasant," Monty said again, laughing.

"Never thought you were the unpleasant one," said Alvin, trying to climb up.

"Well, shows you weren't paying attention," said Piers, trying not to laugh as Alvin slipped and fell back down.

"Yeah I was, and I'll tell you what," Alvin started, then froze. The others heard it too, the merriment dying out. The breeze had picked up slowly, rhythmically. Like breath. Alvin's eyes opened wide and he desperately scrambled up the platform. With a rush of hard soled feet and clicking claws the four Deinonychus stormed the opening, easily leaping the platform and trying to cut off the others. Rifles raised and fired at the swift moving bodies, but their movements were too fast, and too nimble. Alvin was caught from behind by the second wave, and thrown bodily into the air screaming. One hooked him with it's sharp clawed feet and with a quick flick tore him in two. Monty saw it, and screamed defiance and anger, unloading his rifle into the two animals that had already starting eating the still screaming torso. Piers tried to shout a warning, but his voice was lost in the deafening reports of the nineteen rifles still firing. From the side one launched itself at Monty, taking his rifle from his arms, removing both hands. He stood in disbelief at the bloody stumps of his wrists before another gripped his unresisting neck in its jaws and snapped his spine. The crack made Edgar cringe, clear even over the gunshots.

They fell back to the steps leading up, forming a semicircle trying to hold back the dinosaurs, that darted like a duck shoot range. Bullets chipped the dirty white tiles, adding dust to the cordite smoke. The two bodies were ignored as to stop and eat made an easy target, but they still took snapped bites as they passed. Piers felt shocked, and scared. Too fast they had gone from happy to terrified, safe to in danger. And he felt they were being played with. The animals couldn't attack or they would be killed. Most had wounds from lucky shots. But the men were trapped by the dinosaurs. To move would make space to let them in. At a loss what to do Piers kept loading full magazines and firing, all to aware soon they would be empty and there was nothing they could do but run. He was about to shout the order when something flashed from the tunnel he had come from, then another flash.

Emerging from the darkness wielding a rifle like none Piers had seen before Chris walked calmly into the light, Marty at his side with his usual rifle. The big, long barrelled gun Chris struggled to carry fired again, taking a massive chunk of masonry from the wall. The animals saw the new attacker, and turned to face him. Chris smiled as if he was enjoying a summer breeze and fired. The first shot vaporised one dinosaur's head, leaving the body still standing. The second hit one in the chest, punching a hole the size of a fist and adding more blood to the walls. A third removed a leg cleanly. As he aimed his forth the animals broke and fled. In four shots, and four seconds Chris had removed the threat.

Still holding the monster gun in front of him Chris leant it on the platforms edge. Piers saw on closer inspection it was mounted to his body by a harness strapped around his chest.

Chris wiped sweat from his face. "Fun."

"Fun?" Piers asked, realising he was shaking.

"Never get to use this much, too big and heavy. Knew the buggers would mount some sort of ambush. Clever things."

Piers just looked at him with vacant eyes. Chris saw the mutilated bodies of Alvin and Monty. Sadness clouded his cheerful face.

"Who?" he asked.

Piers looked at the bodies, as if trying to work it out. "Monty and little Al. Stupid! All my bloody fault!"

Chris undid the harness, leaving the big gun on the edge, and swung himself up. He took Piers by the shoulders and to everyone it looked like he was ready to shake Piers, or kiss him. Instead he just stared solidly into his eyes.

"Rubbish. You were ambushed. With numbers like that you did bloody well to lose only two. This is not a perfect life. We will lose more, suffer more pain, but if we fall apart now we fail." Chris was still looking into Piers's grief, but speaking to everyone. "So we do what we have to do, we fight. Kill the bastards and go home heroes. They are honoured dead. We should all be so lucky to die like they did." Chris dropped his hands and grunted as he hefted the big gun, and climbed the steps up.

Marty passed Piers, who hadn't moved.

"Speaking personally I'd rather die in a warm bed with a warm woman, but hey ho," he said and followed Chris. Piers dropped his head, unable to face the men behind him. Sensing the massive drop in morale Edgar gave soft orders, organising the men to clear up the two bodies, and cover their exit. When he turned back to get Piers he saw with horror he was gone.

On the surface Chris slung the big gun into the back of the Land Rover and tried to catch his breath. Marty tried to hide his amusement at Chris' exertion.

"You can stop giggling as well, kiddo," Chris said, not looking in Marty's direction.

"Hey, I done nothing," said Marty, hands spread.

"Nothing my arse," said Chris. "Laughing at an old man."

"Only when he's funny."

"I think, old friend, I am getting past it." Chris dropped his head, examining his boots absently.

"Never. You'll be doing this until you die," said Marty, uncomfortable with Chris' lapse back into self depression.

"That is exactly what I'm worried about. We can all do heroics but that gets you killed. A warm bed with a warm woman. Good plan I think."

"Maybe, but where do we find the warm bed?"

Chris looked up at Marty, and burst out laughing at his bemused face. He slung an arm around the younger man's shoulders and drew him closer.

"You're right, as usual, kiddo. Where is our warm beds? Need a scrub, a sleep and some food."

The others finally made it up, Edgar bringing up the rear at near a sprint, panic on his red face. Chris picked it up instantly, grabbing his rifle from the side of the car and meeting him on the top step.

"What?" he asked, rifle aimed into the darkness.

"Piers," Edgar gasped.

"What about him?" asked Marty.

"He's, he's gone."

"Where?" asked Chris. Edgar didn't answer. Chris shook him with one hand. "Where!"

Edgar pointed back down. "There. He was on the platform where you had spoken to him, then when I turned back he was gone."

Chris cursed in pure villager making even Marty blush. Looking at Marty Chris' face went hard.

"We go get him. Stupid sod's gone duck hunting, and these ducks will love that."

Marty nodded, grabbed some full magazine from the others and they plunged down the steps, two at a time.

Piers felt stupid, ashamed and terrified. He had felt anger like he had never known. He wanted only to remove these things from his city, to make them pay for the lives of his men. So he had run into the tunnel after them like a stupid child. And now he was there, in the dark, with no help, no support, and probably surrounded by them. He was going to die because of his own stupidity. Fear soaked his jacked with sweat, making him smell even stronger. His rifle shook in fumbling hands, rattling loudly. All he wanted to do was curl up into a ball and cry until his mother came to take him away. The thought made him actually cry. His mother was long gone, died shortly after he had been born, but he thought often of her. His father, remarried to the beauty from a successful manufacturing family, had spoken only good things of her before some mystery illness took him too. Making them proud was what drove Piers on, and now he had thrown it all away.

Pausing to try to calm himself Piers struggled to make sense of what was around him. The tunnel was the same as the others, but seemed different. He could sense or feel no other presence there, not after the attack. Blood dripped darkly on the floor, giving him a scattered trail to follow. Slowly he recognised features around him. The next opening couldn't be far. Better to come up from there, get to the surface and walk back as a brave Hunter, than scurry back the way he had come like a scared child.

His mind made up Piers raised his rifle in steady hands and walked slowly forwards. Making slow sweeps with the barrel he moved on, until the trail of blood stopped. Crouching to inspect the dusty floor the blood had ended as if the wounded animals had turned away, but there were no openings for them to go through. Puzzled Piers explored the tunnel ahead and behind the end of the trail, then back again. He could see nowhere they could have gone. With a burst of new horror he looked up, but the ceiling was solid and unoccupied. With a final gesture of futility Piers leant on the wall and sighed. And vanished.

Chris lead, Marty walking backwards behind. The blood trail, the boot marks of Edgar's group coming, and Piers's going were easy sign for him to follow. He smelt nothing new, or felt anything was wrong. They heard a short shout, almost of surprise that sounded like Piers, but resisted the urge to run. Keeping their methodical walk they found the end of the trail. Marty kept watch while Chris searched.

"Ok, this one's new on me," he said eventually.

"How come?" asked Marty, still peering into the darkness.

"Blood comes down here, as you'd expect from that much lead flying in there. Pack runs down here, then nothing. Prints in and out. Piers was here too, walked all over looking for the end of the trail, then vanished too."

Marty joined Chris looking at the confusing patterns on the dust. The blood did indeed stop here, and it was over the prints of a line of men, but under the prints of just one. Chris paced back and forth, avoiding walking on the marks, tracing the movements of Piers. He spent twenty minutes bent double as he walked, before finishing up where Piers had leant on the wall. A small, man shaped damp patch showed on the tiled wall. Chris took a long time inspecting the wall that to Marty looked like any other area in the tunnel. In the gloom it was hard to see much, but Chris saw more with his fingers. Marty almost jumped when the latch clicked and the metal door creaked open. Flashing a bright smile Chris took his rifle and headed inside.

To Piers it looked unimaginable. He was hidden in an old control room, about thirty feet above the floor. Once through the door and into the long corridor splattered with blood he had followed the animals through another metal door double hinged so it swung both ways. Faced with a massive open area Piers ducked behind some machinery, and spied the metal steps leading up. Always aiming to gain the high ground he slipped up the steps and into the control room. The large windows were intact, but dirty. Through them he could only stare at what he saw. He nearly screamed when the door open, flinging himself to the floor, rifle raised.

"You know how bad it is to shoot your boss?" asked Chris, un fazed by the shaking gun pointed at him. Piers slowly lowered the gun. "Better," Chris smiled, and knelt beside him, looking through the glass. Marty joined him and together with Piers when he had risen from the floor they stared.

"Well," said Marty absently, "you don't see that everyday.

Chapter Eighteen

The space must have been for maintenance and storage of massive lorries, with massive metal wheels, and rusted smooth bodies, like brown snakes. They sat on the metal rails, and Chris realised they had ran along the metal bars sunk into the floor in the tunnels. The cars had flat ends, but curved roofs so they fitted neatly with the tunnel ceilings. They had no windows left, but there was broken glass all around, and flaking red paint on the ends of the cars. A lump of metal flanked by two flat pieces either side was at chest height, most likely for connecting them together. There were around ten massive cars the size of one of the convoy trucks. But the amazing thing was the occupants.

The nest had relocated here. They had no food stored, but the place was perfect. With massive steel doors behind them leading to the tunnels, and no other way out they were protected. Marty spotted a bent door, barely big enough for a dinosaur to get through. He nudged Chris, who nodded. He'd seen it. And it would be heavily guarded and protected. It was a perfect spot. Only one way in or out they had control over the area nicely. It would be hard to get to the nest past the sentries.

Piers had wandered around the office area, sifting through the piles of dusty papers on the desks. Frowning he looked to Chris with an apologetic look.

"Can you read these shapes?" he asked quietly.

"Sure," Chris whispered, and tore himself away from the dirty window. Picking a stack at random he blew the dust off and tried to read. Most of it was faded, dirty with words so hard to read Chris had to squint in the dim light.

"Well," asked Piers. Marty had taken position at the door, just in case. There was no sign of any animal getting up there, but it paid to take precautions.

"Looks like some sort of maintenance schedule for what they call a tube train. These were pulled for inspection. The others are in a depot outside the city. No idea where. What's the locals name for this place?"

"Nobody's ever been here," said Piers.

"And returned," added Marty. Chris shot him a look.

"I mean," Chris said, "the city. We always called it the city in the plains."

Piers frowned for a moment. "We never do. It's home to us. Nobody leaves so we don't have to say where we live as a city. The oldies say Laden but I think they just made that up. Why?"

Chris held up one of the lower pieces of paper, it's words clearer.

"Says: City Of London Underground Transport Department on here. Guess this is the old city of London, not Laden."

"So it has a name," said Marty, half out the door. "So what? Is there nothing of use?"

"Yes!" hissed Chris. "A map of the tunnels. Got two actually. One is a load of lines, colour coordinated with names of stops for this underground train. The other looks more like the tunnels themselves. Names, access ducts, maintenance hatches and the electricity stations."

"This place had power?" Marty asked.

"Yep, and a clever system. Struggling with the big words, but it seems they used the river and wind to power it. Some new method it says here. Big thing in those days. Wonder if we could fix it?"

"Serious?" asked Marty, still hanging half out the door. "What for?"

"Think about it. A real transport system. Plus if the

lights and stuff work we can blast these things out of the dark to where we can see them." Chris tailed off slightly as he read deeper. "You are kidding," he breathed.

"What?" asked Piers, trying to read over his shoulder, even though the symbols and shapes meant nothing to him. Chris had seen electrical diagrams in the bunker, from the old days, and slowly learnt what they meant.

"They have cameras to see everything," Chris said. "A camera is a device that saves an image and sends it to a monitor that displays it. Means you can see something as if you were there, but you don't have to be."

"Sounds like magic," Piers said.

"Maybe, but it would solve our problem perfectly. See them, find them, kill them. I have radios so we can talk people to where they need to go, but it says here there is a system to speak to people from the main control room."

"Where is it?" asked Marty.

"Got it on this map. The generator, the relay stations, the diagnostics room, the logistics room. Everything. Piers?"

"Yeah?"

"Any inventors or electric specialists in this city?"

Piers thought. "Not really. We know electricity exists, but not for much use. Lightning is electricity, and some have made lights that glow from it, but they don't last long and kill you if you change them. The convoy trucks use electricity to run the engines, and I heard a port near the city has an electric crane. If the before time had electricity they died with the knowledge to use it."

Chris flipped through the sheets energetically, making a small cloud of dust. Finally he found what he was looking for.

"Aha! Nailed it. Says here there is a training room with hard copy reference books. We can find it all there."

"So what next, boss?" asked Marty.

"Next, we make old Precious one very happy mayor."

The Attendant bowed to the departing man as he stormed from the office without acknowledging him. Ignoring the highly offensive gesture the Attendant maintained his composure and was about to close the double doors when Precious called him.

"Yes, sire?" he asked.

"Ah, a nasty little fellow, he was," smiled Precious, then his face fell, an extra chin formed to join the others.

"He is right though. We have a problem. May I ask you something, unusual?"

The Attendant was shocked. He still hid his feelings under a mask of efficient subservience but having never been asked for advice from his master he was taken aback.

"Naturally, sire. I am here for you."

Calmed by the man's smooth speech and calm face Precious almost smiled. He did go red in uncomfortable embarrassment.

"The thing is, we have a problem. We are making too little. No matter how fast we make our products, we can't keep with demands. If this carries on we will have serious supply issues. Naturally it helps raise prices and desirability, but it's cutting into profits. I hear little from the lower classes, but I know there are some who mend, and some who create. Have you heard of such men?"

The Attendant was such a man, who had a table littered with inventions in his small chambers next to the office. Keeping caution on his side he smiled and said, "I may have heard of some, sire, but what help could they be?"

Precious coughed. "They could be of great use." He looked at the man in the eye. "Imagine it. If I could help usher in a new era, of faster production, more profitable production. Nobody could out produce me."

"Your position would be secure, and you would be a prominent figure in our history," said the Attendant.

Precious beamed. "Exactly! Well said. I agree, and I need your help to find the right man."

The Attendant, still stood by the doors with his hands clasped behind his back tried to act a puzzled face, as if searching for the answer he already knew. After a brief pause he smiled.

"Maybe, sire, if you ran a contest? With a suitable reward to the winner. If someone could design, and build a miniature scale production machine, then you can choose the best."

"Perfect. Set it up, and spread the word. An initiative contest. Large reward for the winner, and a place on the new innovation committee. Good man." Precious dismissed the Attendant with a wave and pulled out a new sheet of paper, then looked at it in the light of the big window, thinking. The Attendant smiled, and closed the door. He nearly walked into Chris, had his attuned senses to visitors not been triggered.

"Greeting, Mr Spencer," he said.

"Old podgy Precious in?" Chris asked.

The Attendant suppressed a smile. "He is in, sir, and

busy I fear. Did you have an appointment?"

Chris pulled a face. "Of course not, but he will want to see me. Gonna make him a happy bunny."

"Happy?"

"Yep. Found a way to make electricity, to use it, and to make it safe for every home."

Seeing a golden opportunity laid in his lap the Attendant grabbed it.

"He is busy, but please explain it to me. I may be able to help. You see, he has created a new innovation council and I think this will be the perfect project for him."

Chris knew a ploy when he saw one. "Well, us outsiders should stick together," he said, and sat with the Attendant by the small desk.

Chapter Nineteen

Later that day the mayor was surprised by a loud knock. He called the Attendant on the tube, but he didn't appear. Muttering Precious lifted his bulk from the chair and opened the door himself. There stood the Attendant, looking sheepish, and Chris looking smug, more than normal.

"What is this?" asked Precious.

"A deputation," said Chris when the Attendant didn't speak.

"A deputation?" repeated Precious.

"Yep, you see, we have the solution to your problem." Chris swept past Precious and sat in the mayor's chair. From the other side of the big desk the room seemed tiny, the large window casting his shadow onto the piles of notes on the dark wood desk. Chris absently sifted through them. "We are here to offer you a chance to make your big mark."

Precious took the papers from Chris and gave him a look that wilted flowers. "And how, may I ask, are you intending to accomplish this? Magic?"

"Nope," smiled Chris. "All I need is a pass to leave town, and some fuel."

"Fuel? It's hard for us to get it, without giving it away. Do you know how expensive it is, or how long it takes the farms to grow it?"

"I used most of mine helping you and training your staff."

The mayor shook his head, and with surprising

strength lifted Chris bodily from his chair. After smoothing his robes and checking his thinning hair Precious resumed his disgusted stare.

"Do you have any idea where our fuel comes from?" he asked.

"Not a clue," said Chris, "but I know where it's going."

"It has to be grown with special seeds, then refined before we can use it. Each convoy brings a tanker full, just for the return trip. It's very expensive and hard to get. I can't afford your usage on top."

"Oh well," Chris said cheerfully, "Time I went home. I have only enough to get back. Good luck, Tubs." He patted the mayor on the shoulder, ignoring his flinch, and headed for the door.

"Wait!"

Chris paused, trying to take the smile from his face, and failing.

"Ok." Precious sighed theatrically. "You can have some fuel, but I want to know why you need it."

"I can help, sire," said the Attendant.

"You?"

"Yes, sire. You see, I have been inventing for years in

my chambers, and have managed to make a small scale wind power turbine that can light a small electric bulb. The system Mr Spencer has discovered in the tunnels ran most of the old city, however it needs someone with skills in electricity beyond my meagre abilities to restore it. Mr Spencer had the intelligent idea of finding this man and offering him employment repairing the city's electrical supply. It means we will have the first fully electric city, with powered machines to greatly improve production, and profits."

The last words hung in the air like a falcon. Precious had gone from amazed to enthralled. Gold poured before his mind's eye and he looked almost besotted.

"You can do this?" he asked.

"I believe it can be done," said the Attendant.

"Go to it. You are now in the service of the city Mr, forgive me, I never learned your name."

The Attendant smiled. "I am Mr John Malcolm, sire, and I accept your offer of employment."

"Good, Malcolm, good." Precious made a note in the litter of paper. "How do you intend to find this person?"

"He is in the coastal town where our fish is delivered," John said. "He is, as far as I am aware, attempting to make it last until it can be delivered here fresh as when it still swam."

"Good, Malcolm. Go get him, bring him back and then find someone who can make machines that make things very quickly and cheaply."

"Ahead on that," said John.

"Excellent, well, don't let me detain you. The Attendant will show you out, oh." Precious managed to blush under his red pallor. "I will need to hire a new man. You know your way, Malcolm."

"Yes, sire." John bowed and left. Chris shot Precious a chirpy smile and followed. Precious unloaded a full magazine of hate into the back of the tattered camouflaged jacket.

Outside the sun was setting, casting red glares on the white walls and making the city seem draped in a crimson shroud. John let out a breath that seemed held for life, unhooked his white robe collar and gave a weak smile to Chris. In his plain white gown with no shoes he still looked the object of superior servitude. As tall as Chris, and half as wide he looked like a tree bent in the wind. The white of his clothes only made his face seem paler.

"Well, that went better than I expected," John said.

"True," Chris agreed. "Old tubby is a bit keen on cash and that got him good a proper."

John smiled and looked up to the large window high above him.

"All I ever knew is up there, or out there," he said, looking to the high wall circling the city.

"We both know out there," said Chris. "And out there is where we are going. Know this bloke by name or sight?"

"Neither. Only by reputation. Should be easy enough to find. Town isn't big."

"I hope not," said Chris, leading John away from the courtyard. "I don't feel like a long drive, and old Precious won't let us have much fuel."

"He will, when his official Attendant signs the chitty," said John, straightening his robes. Chris smiled and slapped him on the back, nearly sending John flying.

"You're all right, kiddo. Let's gas up and go."

Chapter Twenty

Having filled the Land Rover, and a trailer with a large black fuel tank in it Chris, Marty and John left the strong, high gates behind. Marty actually cheered as they left the still heat from the city, warmed like an oven since the rains had left. Feeling the cooler breeze on their faces, the smell of grass, dust, animal waste and flowers, they followed the high, off grey walls of the city. They had left by the east gate, on the short convoy route to the fishing town. This route was little used as most products were floated down the river in the spring and autumn months, and carried in carts or small convoys in summer. Winter closed the route, as it did with many others, when the broken tarmac and dirt became impassable. The high walls loomed like an unhappy parent, people on the tops walking the sentry ledge looked tiny, watching them leave. Nobody left out of choice, except the convoy drivers, who were well paid, but tended to live in other cities.

The dirt road turned away from the city and wound along beside the river. Some parts were good with smooth stretches of decent surface, even tarmac with white lines still there. Others were potholed and nearly impossible. Chris wondered how people managed without a high car like the Land Rover, and worried for the old cars suspension. He feared the decades or maybe even centuries, it had lain with the others in the bunker would have weakened it badly. It had never failed him yet, but it had been used and abused for many years since he found it. One of the priorities Chris made sure of was the knowledge to repair it. He had stripped and rebuilt three, his included, before he left the bunker, ensuring every part was good. But without the fuel it was made for, and no new parts and oils it was only a matter of time. The Land Rover bore the scars of a hard life; one side was deeply dented when a large herbivore had flipped it escaping one of his traps, another on the square front from an unfortunate brush with an Allosaurus that broke the plastic grille and made the lights look slightly cross eyed. The engine had recently begun to rattle slightly, with some blue smoke behind. It was needing another rebuild, but parts were still in the bunker.

Marty didn't have these fears. He was both happy, and sad. Happy because he was back outside, in the fresh air, and the breeze. He always felt like a drifter, blown where the wind sends him, never staying anywhere long. He was sad because he missed the luxuries of the city, water that tasted clean, streets without any dirt at all, friendly people when they got to know you, and friendly ladies. Marty smiled at the memory of the thin gauze they wore to signify sexual readiness, and how soon he learnt the customs of courting. In a big city he could hide, but the walls kept him from escaping angry fathers for deflowering their daughters.

John looked over the flat bonnet of the car in the back seat as if he could see the town already. He had forgotten what the outside was like, and how much he missed it. Living in the city had dampened his senses, but not his spirit. He had no doubt his offer of employment would tempt the man he sought to help him, elevating John to the level of business, no more a mere servant. He looked to the future, and the town, with great excitement, even if he was looking in the wrong direction due to the rivers turns.

They passed several small villages, their walls high and thick. Small farms were scattered around, each with similar defences. Chris cast his experienced eye over another village, and half turned in his seat, keeping a watch where he was driving.

"Hey, John? Where you from?"

"Near here, actually," John called back over the noise of the car. "If we went past the town we're aiming for then you'd find my old place."

"So why the walls?"

John looked puzzled. "Walls? For protection."

"I know that. But they're bigger than most walls we see back west, and you have farms away from the villages. Just wondering why."

"Ah. The river," John said, as if that explained all. Chris shot him a look that showed it didn't. "There are bandits here, raiders I think you called them. They use barges and boats they have found or stolen. Some are fishing boats they catch, others barges towed behind sail boats taking trade and fish to or from the smokers."

"Smokers?" asked Marty.

"They hang the fish in a tall building and light fires with green wood. The smoke preserves the fish."

"I remember something about that," said Marty, distracted.

Chris almost ran the car off the road. Cursing he swung the four wheel drive back onto the dirt. "You remember what?" he asked.

"Just fish, in a high shed like a fat chimney, in smoke so thick you can hardly see them." Marty looked to the river on their left, and sighed. Chris knew to leave him be. Ever since losing his memories however it happened Marty had struggled, like a man with no history. Chris had tried to help, but it only made Marty angry and frustrated. They both decided to let him remember over time, which rarely happened. John sensed the tension and kept quiet.

Chris saw a little later on one of John's sail barges. It looked almost serene as it drifted by on the breeze. Each barge was about forty feet long, and ten wide. Square beamed and with one tow rope fore and one aft they followed the sail boat like ducks. The sail boat itself was shorter, with a narrow hull, almost like a feather, with one large thick mast hanging a wide, patched sail. All made from wood they floated like twigs on a current. Chris could see men on the sail boat, and some on the barges. They crossed to each by ropes laid from barge to barge like a bridge.

Marty also saw the boat, and kept his eyes on it. Even when they turned away as the river bent, he spun around in his seat to see it. Chris noticed, and kept silent, bracing in case Marty jumped from the car. When a cluster of trees and ruined houses from the before finally hid the boat Marty turned back and sat in intense silence. Passing more derelict houses and buildings Chris felt his heart beat speed up. Perfect bandit area, with blind corners and close cover. The road cut through the dead town, leaving the river to cut out a meander. Marty woke from his thoughts and without a word slid his rifle from the holder behind his seat as Chris kept going. John felt useless in the back, but touched the big gun fastened down to the roll cage it was fitted to. The relief was almost solid when they left the edge of the ruins and headed back into the open.

"Many animal attacks here?" Chris asked John.

"Not really, we never seem to be affected by them. We heard stories as kids, bogey men who would eat you if you misbehaved, or went out alone at night. It was bandits more than anything else. They'd snatch children even in daylight. Good child labour helped them, and eventually the child would become a raider too. Sometimes they raped or killed them, just to keep the fear up."

"Nobody helped you?" asked Marty.

"Nobody. We had nobody to turn to. They were in

groups of at least ten and usually thirty. They'd come ashore out of sight and sneak in. In those sort of numbers you could do little. Just hide and hope. Our village was hit once, after I left. There wasn't much untouched there, or intact. What won't burn, they break. The people were either burned, or beaten, the choice women kept for slaves, children for work and the men killed before their families to break their spirit." John looked out to the river, far to the north, snaking like a silver chain in the sun. He shivered and pulled a coat on to hide it. Chris felt a chill, and knew it wasn't the weather.

"Sucks," said Marty. "No help, no hope." He looked to Chris. "Maybe somebody should help them."

Chris caught the look and smiled his nasty grin. "Maybe, if they are unlucky."

"That won't help," said John from the depths of his big coat. "They live on the river. Only a boat could reach them, and none are big enough or fast enough to get there before they scatter."

"Another different battlefield," muttered Chris and squinted through the heat haze on the horizon. Ahead, vague in the distortion, a large, strong looking dull grey wall rose from the ground. It almost looked like the city, so much so Marty was about to accuse Chris of getting lost, a rare occurrence. As they got closer differences appeared. The walls were lower, less well laid out, and more patched. The road led straight to a high alcove in the wall, with thick wooden gates half open, and a wooden barrier stopping traffic.

"That is?" asked Marty.

"That's it," confirmed John. "Gilliam town."

Chapter Twenty-One

Gilliam town was smaller than Chris expected, but that was mostly down to the difference between the town and the city. Unlike the big city the town seemed built in rings, the outer being the walls with houses built against it, then the richer looking dwellings with small gardens, vegetable plots and even stables. The inner rings were even more elaborate, ending in some large, plain buildings that John identified as storehouses. In the very centre was a large oval space which today was a bustling market, with fish traders jostling and shouting from stalls, carts and even some motorised trucks. The road in and out went east to west, and wound through the town, rather than go direct. It circled the market to free up traffic flow, and as they drove around the crowds Marty darted from the car into the mass of people. Chris slammed on the brakes, causing a cart behind to stop quickly, the horse pulling it nearly head butting the car. Chris stood on his seat, one hand steadying himself on the roll frame. He soon saw Marty, being unusually tall, weaving through to a fish stall. He held out a small coin, and got a hook of fish, which he slung on his back and pushed his way to the car. Hanging the hook of five silvery fish in the back near John Marty offered a sheepish smile to Chris, who kept his stare, ignoring the increasingly frustrated carter behind, then pulled away. John examined the fish.

"Trout, I think. Looks smoked properly, smells ok too."

"Edible raw?" asked Chris.

"Sure, just be careful for bones," said John, handing an oily fish to Chris, who drove one handed down the windy road, gnawing on the fish which slipped in his grubby hand. Marty looked hurt at the loss of a fish, then took the one offered by John, realising they were not going to last long. Chris liked fish, so rare a treat, and having not stopped all day they were hungry.

"The town hall is just ahead, but we want a small brewer behind it," said John, pointing out identical streets. Chris hurried his fish, spitting bones, then dropped in on Marty's lap and hefted the big wheel. The old Land Rover was perfect for rough ground, but in the narrow streets made for pedestrians and horses it was a tight fit. Twice they heard the shriek of metal catching on stone. Chris was soaked in sweat when they finally found the brewer.

It was a small alcove, with chairs outside, and the smell of stale beer and sawdust hanging like perfume. A hole in the alcove served as a bar, with shutters to close the outside world away at home time. The chairs were all wooden, and patched. They spread out to near the other end of the street and Chris had to stop and kill the engine.

"Now?" he asked.

"Now," said John, "we ask the keeper if he has seen the guy we need."

John jumped from the car and headed to the bar. Chris motioned Marty to stay with the car, and followed. The end of summer sun bounced off the whitened walls of the street, the narrow enclosure making it feel even warmer. Chris felt ready for a drink, even though alcohol was unusual in his diet. Most small villages made enough to eat, without luxuries like distilleries. John was already at the bar, perched on a ledge that ran below the wooden topped opening. The keeper was taking his order, sweating profusely under his smart white robe and black waistcoat. Two large clay mugs appeared from below the bar, filled with dirty brown coloured beer from a larger jug. John held it to his face like a precious flower, inhaled deeply, and smiled, eyes closed. Without a word he sipped the frothy beer, nearly falling backwards as he groaned in pleasure. Finally opening his eyes he looked at Chris and went pink.

"So long since a mug of Old Skanky I forgot how good it was."

Chris smiled, and sipped his beer. It was good, warm, sweet and slightly woody. To the surprise of the keeper and John Chris threw his head back and downed the mug. Placing it gently on the wood he belched loudly and grinned.

"Not bad, could do with more kick though," he said. Without a hint the keeper refilled his mug.

"Now, kind keeper," said John, "we are looking for the man who plays with electricity."

"Why?"

"We have a job for him."

The keeper looked around like a spy. "He is never here," he said slowly and deliberately. "I don't see him, or know him." He turned away and re stacked some mugs on the back wall. John was about to reach for him when a soft noise behind made Chris hold out a hand. Without moving his head Chris soundlessly counted down, then dropped to the floor, rolled and knelt, pistol raised. He saw only Marty beside the Land Rover, but hidden behind him, a shadow of a man, the glint of a blade clear in the reflected sun. Another crouched by the flat front of the Land Rover. Marty looked apologetic, and chewed his fish. Chris lowered the pistol and cursed.

The man facing him was short, almost comically so, besides Chris' six foot three. He was also a lot slimmer, looking more apologetic then aggressive. The pistol was old, and showed rust on it's tarnished stubby barrel from the salt air. The black rifled opening quivered as the man held it at arms length. His companion behind Marty was taller, but not any better built, his polished blade looked more like a fish gutters knife then assassins tool. Realising the mild threat imposed Chris held back a laugh.

"And you are?" he asked.

"None of your business," said the nervous man, shaking slightly.

"And you want?"

"You to leave here."

Chris held his stare, waiting for the man to crack. One trick he used a lot was to make the other person in a confrontation feel uncomfortable, making them make the first move. The man cracked.

"Leave, now please. Ask no questions."

Chris stayed put. The man became increasingly agitated, sweating and glancing to his associate who was already trying to get away from Marty, who was still munching his fish. John leant against the bar, drinking another mug of beer, watching with mild amusement. The man shook the ache from his arm and took better aim, wavering the pistol between Chris' head and chest.

"You know how that works, kiddo?" Chris asked.

"Killed many with this. Your words and guns scare me little."

Chris opened his mouth to speak, made a clicking noise instead, and plucked the gun from the man's hand as if taking a toy from a naughty child. A grunt told him Marty had disarmed the other man. Chris smiled his smile again as the man wilted almost to a cower.

"Not with the safety on, son," Chris said, checking the small guns magazine. "And certainly without bullets. You try to impose them to death?"

The man kept quiet. He knelt down, head bowed, as if waiting for execution. Chris tossed the gun to Marty, who dropped it into the back of the Land Rover.

"Now then, you and me are gonna have a chat," Chris said, sitting in one of the battered chairs, his own pistol in his hand rested on one knee. The man didn't move. Marty stayed by the car, one boot on the back of the other man, equally silent.

"Firstly, why are you here?" The man stayed silent, so Marty put more weight on the man until he grunted.

Chris didn't look, but the man on his knees did.

"I had to tell you to leave," murmured the man.

"Why?" asked Chris, accepting a beer from John.

"Because," said the man.

"Who by?"

"I can't say."

The other man grunted in pain again.

"Pardon?" asked Chris.

"The Sparky," said the man.

"Sparky?" asked John. "The guy who can make electric work?"

"Yes," said the man.

Chris drained the mug, took his and John's to the bar, dropped a scruffy coin on the polished wood and nudged the man with his foot.

"Lead on, then," he said.

They followed in the car, Chris making them walk in front, Marty aiming the big guns dark metal barrel on them. John sat in the passenger seat, mildly amused at the scene. The old Land Rover rattled its way through close, light stone streets. The stone had come from different sources, scavenged from buildings when the before time fell. Patchwork repairs and mismatched stone broke up the colours, making a mottled effect. Houses leaned at crazy angles, with a small vegetable plot behind each. The streets were laid out in a vaguely crosswise pattern, but with waving lines and strange intersections that made the builders make weird shaped houses. All this, and the autumn heat ricocheting from the walls made Chris sweat profusely, soaking his light tunic a darker shade of greens and browns.

As they weaved the streets music, tinny and rough, melded with the heat. The streets were deserted, most being in the market, but some children started following the car, reaching out to touch it as it rumbled over the rough ground. More joined, shouting and laughing. As the music grew louder and more distinct the group grew so the alley behind was filled with kids, pushing to keep up with the slow car. Chris grunted in irritation at the sight in the dirty door mirror, and focused on not clipping any more walls. Marty swung the big gun around to face them, but the kids laughed even more, daring each other to touch the barrel that overhung the rear.

The music stopped, and cheering drowned any attempts to play more. Finding a small square near the outer wall Chris let out a long held breath as the men in front stopped and pointed. The kids, annoyed their game had ended, kicked the back of the car as if trying to get it to move again. Over the square hung a large sheet of sack cloth, supported by the walls around. Under danced and twirled a mass of people all dressed in pure white. In the centre, under a cut out that let the sun beam on them, sat a young couple, both in jet black, on high chairs with ornate arm rests and wing backs. Some young ladies, in grey gowns open at the front and back to their waists, danced around them, twirling. The couple in black sat smiling, the girl with a look of pure joy, the man a look of bemusement.

Chris grabbed one of the men. "Which one?"

The exhausted man shrugged and pointed. "The old one by the bar. It's his sisters daughters day of joining. He will not be happy being disturbed."

Chris cursed and waved the men away, who vanished into the alley after the kids. Marty dropped from the back and leant on the dented panel.

"Plan's boss?" Marty asked.

Chris watched as the musicians raised their instruments, checked the strings and mouthpieces, and instantly dived into another upbeat song. John sat on the flat bonnet, watching the they danced. Marty watched the girls in grey.

"Keep watch on the car, kiddo," said Chris.

"What you doing?" asked Marty, seeing his evening's fun in danger.

"Go introduce myself," said Chris. He took his pistol from his hip holster and passed it to Marty, brushed the road dust from his clothes, and tried to straighten his messy hair, seeing with distaste the grey strands forming a slow advance. Without looking at the shocked pair he walked formally to the rings of dancers, paused, then jumped in, joining them. Standing out like a stone in sandpit he twirled, swirled and whirled around, sweat dripping from his brow, but a smile lighting his face. Marty saw for the first time the man he had been before he met Chris. The man with a life so cruelly taken away. John didn't know Chris well, hardly seeing him save when he saw the mayor. But he couldn't help tapping a foot to the beat of the players, and let himself be swept away with the crowd when one ring came too close. Marty settled himself on the drivers seat as best he could, loosened his tunic and nibbled absently on his last fish.

Chris danced like the best, even getting allowed into the innermost ring, traditionally for family and close friends, near enough to the joining party that danced around the joined pair. With precision and flair he kicked his booted heels amongst bare footed ladies, stomped with soft soled men, and daintily danced with fair skinned women. Their flowing, open attire made a plethora of patterns and shapes, like a wind swirling dust. They spun around the happy pair, the hot air fragranced with herbs, spices, cooked meat and sweat. As the sun slowly sank below the western buildings the tempo slowed. The couple stood, held hands and stepped down to dance their own dance, slow and sensual. The others stood around them, then slowly joined, making a gentle swaying. Chris found himself with one of the joining party, her brief gown smudged slightly by his dirty clothes. Marty held back a cheer. John was with an elderly lady, more conservatively dressed, but still dancing the slow fertility dance.

A hand landed on Chris' shoulder with the clear message it could hold a lot firmer if needed. Chris elegantly bowed to his partner, turned and followed the massive man who had stopped him. He led to the bar, where his escort stood beside the old man who had been pointed out to him.

"You dance well, stranger," he said, with a voice like gravel.

"You throw an excellent party," Chris replied with grace. "My compliments to your players."

"You are kind, but unwanted. I know your name, Spencer, and your reputation." The man looked past at Marty, trying subtly to attract on of the grey dressed girls. "And that of your, friend. It is kind you should show my niece such skill, but not like this. Please leave."

"I can't. I am here as envoy for Mayor Precious."

The man scoffed and sat down. There was no other chairs for Chris. "That fat fool? We laugh at him here, in his little office, with his little men making little decisions. Here we live our lives properly. We work hard, dance hard, love hard. Much like you, Hunter. However here to follow rules. You don't. I have nothing to say to you, or the fat ruler of yours. In honest truth, you disappoint me. I heard you were a free spirit, a leaf on the wind as it were. Not a lap dog."

Chris held his cool smile. "I may be escorting old Tubbs's speaker, but I work *for* him, not under him. His price is getting dearer by the day, but that's nothing to do with you. You like sparks, electricity? They have the ability to use it, but no idea how. You wanna really make use of sparks you come with us, you don't then stay here." Chris rose, bowed deeply and turned away. After a couple of steps he turned back. "By the way, don't send kids to do a man's work." Chris slipped his hand into his sweat soaked tunic and pulled the rusty pistol from a chest holster. Dropping it on a wicker table he turned away and walked around the still swaying group. The old man picked up the pistol, grimaced in disgust at the warm wetness, and flicked it to one of his guards. He watched Chris push Marty over to the other seat, gesture John into the back, and drive with some difficulty out of the square.

"It seems Mr Spencer is a resourceful man," the man said softly to himself. "Interesting."

Chapter Twenty-Two

Chris rolled out of his hammock, did a half flip in the air any cat would be proud of, and landed on one knee on the dirt floor. The sunny weather had given them the chance to sleep alfresco and enjoy a starlit ceiling. Marty was still snoring in his bed, the strings straining under the weight of him and two party girls he'd managed to find. Chris smiled at the thought that Marty could find pretty girls anywhere. John was sleeping silently sprawled over the flat bonnet of the car, drooling. Chris looked around briefly, then unzipped his flies and pissed against a hut. The walls of Gilliam loomed blotchy above him, still on the inside of their protective strength. After the party Chris decided to make camp, and return home the following morning. The electrical genius seemed too full of himself to help, so they would work it out themselves. Chris knew some electrics. When he found the bunker he had to learn to read, then how to repair the equipment, all of which aside from basic weapons, used some electronics. He didn't understand it, but he could fix it. Marty was best with his hands, almost gifted. The girls were just his way of keeping those long fingers nimble.

Shaking it off Chris zipped himself back up, checked the pistol strapped to his hip and coughed loudly. John rolled over, and off the bonnet with a startled oomph. Marty stopped mid snore, the girls shrieking and dropping like pink bombs from the hammock. They gathered their open dresses around themselves and fled barefoot. Marty watched them go with disappointment, then out of habit checked his pistol and rifle. John stood, dusting himself off while Chris lit a small fire to boil water.

"So, the plan, boss?" asked Marty, watering Chris' puddle himself.

"We clean up, pack up, and sod off." Chris dropped a match into the small cone of sticks and leapt backwards as the fuel soaked wood caught with a small mushroom cloud. John stifled a laugh. Marty didn't.

"That's it?" asked John, lips quivering.

"That's it. We came, we spoke, we were turned away. Leave him to play deadbeat, we have a job to do, and it's taking far longer than it should. Marty."

"Yeah?" said Marty, pouring water from a bottle into a metal pot.

"Three S's then check the car. I need the lay of the

land." Chris rubbed his stubble, searched his pack for a small cut throat razor and stropped it on his boot. When the water boiled he used a dirty rag to warm and wet his face, then dragged it over his chin. Marty took it after and when Chris had gone he put it in the water for a while, then shaved himself. John watched, fascinated. The city men were all clean shaved, sometimes shaving daily, but never with such a razor. Mostly they used multiple bladed contraptions that could shave cheese into thin slices. Marty caught him watching, and offered the blade, handle first. John took it, and studied the blade with fear and amazement.

"Never used one before?" Marty asked.

"Nope. Always used a shave tool," said John.

"Simple, when you know how, deadly if you don't."

Marty put the rag on John's chin and carefully shaved him. After they cleaned up, and Chris returned, taking a folding shovel from a tool box built into the side of the car.

"Shiny," Chris said, looking at the smooth faces. He shouldered the shovel and left. John looked questioningly at Marty, who laughed.

"Three S's," he said. "Shave, scrub, and squat. He's on the squat stage, scrubbed in the well over there."

"The shovel?"

"Not nice leaving it on the surface," said Marty, and he turned away to prep the car.

The open back of the old Land Rover was basic even by rural standards. The metal floor was scuffed and worn, everything under a layer of dust. The sides were stepped to cover the back wheels, and various storage lockers were built into the gaps. The centre of the load bed was taken up mostly by the mount for the big gun, a heavy tripod bolted to the floor. It spun through mounts in the roll frame to allow the user to spin 360 degrees, and stay fairly secure. A fold down canvas seat beside was the only comfort when travelling. On the flat bonnet over the headlights was two packs, containing ammo, food and extra clothing for emergencies. The windscreen was gone, only the mounts left. On the passenger side a mount for a smaller gun let the passenger have some offensive capability, while the driver had only the wheel in front of him. The doors were also removed. The stripped down, no frills look made the Land Rover look menacing and dangerous. As Marty pulled apart and replaced weapons and kit from it nothing was done to reduce the threatening look.

Chris wandered back as Marty was finishing. Tossing the shovel to him Chris flipped a catch in the grille and opened the bonnet. Inside the old diesel engine lurked like a muddy fish in a shallow pond. Chris ignored the brown slime, and the black streaks of oil, pulling dipsticks and checking levels. John realised these two misfits were far from happy go lucky wanderers, but actual professionals, taking care of their equipment, and relying on each other, almost to the subconscious level to be there for them. He felt more then a little jealousy.

Marty came back, and passed the shovel to John, who looked from it to Marty, and back to the shovel. Heading around the back of the hut he saw two patches of freshly dug earth, and made a hole next to them. When he came back Chris glanced up from the big gun, while Marty was feeding belt linked rounds into a box mounted to the side of the smaller gun.

"Flushed it?" Chris asked.

"And put the seat down?" added Marty.

John looked confused, then realised the joke, offered a weak smile and folded the shovel. Marty took it and put it into a locker. Happy with the big gun Chris slapped the loading cover down, cocked it and double checked the safety. Swinging from the top of the roll frame into the drivers seat he ignored the cloud of dust from the ripped vinyl seats and turned the key. Marty slid in beside him, leaving John to make as best he could in the back.

Bouncing through the narrow streets Chris had scoped out an easy route to the west gate, and back to the city. He drove with a grim face, no humour or joking. Marty knew he was concerned, but was sensibly waiting for

Chris to say what was on his mind.

"Trouble in our path," Chris said finally, as the passed the empty market area and sighted the gate.

"Trouble?" Marty asked.

"Big trouble. Seems our prehistoric friends are moving this way, looking for food. Also bandits have been raiding the roads for food to stock up for winter. Best be on our toes."

Marty nodded and rested a hand on the gun in front of him, watching the shadow cast by the low morning sun lead them on. A couple of miles from the town they were through a small patch of trees when Chris suddenly hit the brakes hard, and killed the engine.

"Wha-," John started to speak but Chris hushed him. Marty strained his ears, hearing only the ticking of the engine cooling, and his own breathing. Chris slid from his seat, silently took his rifle from the holder and moved forwards, hunting. Marty shot John a 'stay here' look, took his own rifle and followed, a little behind and to the left of Chris. Feeling exposed in the open road John pulled on a green plastic feeling helmet hanging from the big gun, found the safety and held the two big handle s on the back, thumb poised over the button.

Chris moved with practised skill and stealth towards the sound, the hairs on his back sticking up like a cat. He smelt, and felt, something was wrong. He knew without looking Marty was near him, and with rifle held in his shoulder, finger on the trigger guard he moved at a half crouch off the dirt and tarmac road into the long grass. Marty followed, keeping low. Slowly the vague noises grew louder, shouting, swearing, pain, until the began to split into individual voices. They stopped near the edge of the grass, where the road had turned almost back on itself. Through the browning blades of grass they saw a crowd of scruffy, unkempt men pulling things off a metal cart, tearing open backs and boxes, searching the contents, and going back for more. Most were full of clothes or paper, some were wires and strange metal boxes. Two people were on the ground, being questioned by a taller man, just as badly dressed, but with an absurd feathered plumage on a cloak. Chris knew the sight from many previous meetings with raiders and bandits to know who they were, and what they were doing.

The plumaged man held up a fist, and brought it down hard on one of the men, who sprawled on the dirt. He was lifted by another man, who held him and put back into a kneeling position. Words were spoken again, and then the fist. Chris inspected the raiders. None had projectile weaponry, most had clubs or spears. None had anything dangerous to them. He tapped Marty gently, looked him in the eyes, then with a few discreet hand gestures Chris crawled backwards and moved off to the right. Marty did the same, going left. Once in position

Chris gave a cough, making the raiders stop and look around. A whistle made them look harder, as one dropped to the floor, and small hole in his forehead. Two more whistles, two more on the floor. The raiders hefted their clubs, searching for an attacker. More whistles, more fell. The plumaged raider shouted orders, then fell himself. Seeing their leader dead the rest looked to each other, then ran. Marty stayed hidden, reloading his silenced pistol and covering Chris, who made a cautious sweep with his rifle, then moved to the two men on the floor. Once he was sure it was clear he turned the beaten man onto his back.

"Hello," said Chris, smiling. "Changed your mind, did we?"

The electrical expert looked through hooded grey eyebrows and scowled.

Chapter Twenty-Three

In the pure white office of the Mayor, lit by the warm autumn sun, Precious leant over his pile of paperwork, making sure not to drip sweat on the crisp sheets. After Park's removal, Chris' assurance of power for production and a good financial quarter his position was secure, now was the time to make some big choices to strengthen his position, and credit account. He had already used his advanced knowledge of the power supply restoration to arrange several engineers in the city to design him machines that would run on this new free energy, retaining them on his payroll to stop others getting the best. He had also requisitioned in the next convoy extra supplies of sheet steel, lumbar and building materials for his new industry. A little study into the old records made the startling discovery that water from the river could be cleaned with this lost technology making a safe, non intoxicating source of hydration for the city. Precious made sure the best were his, and most had passed through his door this day, signing contracts Precious carefully filled out himself. His new Attendant wasn't as good as the old one, wherever he was now. There was no news from Chris, which mildly concerned Precious, his whole future, the gamble he made on production and supply materials would make him lose face come election time.

A soft knock at the door announced the next visitor. Without looking up Precious knew his guest, called for them to enter, and resumed his next contract. The door whispered open silently, and closed with barely a click. Precious ignored the visitor, having long learnt to let them squirm a little, feel uncomfortable, off guard. He let the metal quill nib scratch on the parchment while he heard the soft breath of the man waiting. Precious felt something wrong, something almost animal inside shouting a warning. Glancing up slightly to the far edge of his desk he saw nothing. Normally guests waited on the little black line on the floor to be addressed, but this visitor had ignored the line, and was not even near the desk. Also a slow shadow moving on his desk melding with his own finally alerted him to the man behind him. He finished his line, laid the quill into it's holder and looked up. The man sat in his armchair beside the door gave a smile that stabbed like ice needles into his heart. The colour of his face, reddened by the warm sun on his back, fell so fast the visitor actually looked under the dark wood desk for a pool of colour. A small pressure on his back told Precious the man behind was holding something against his elegant white gown.

"Surprised to see me?" the man in the chair asked, his voice squeaking.

Precious opened his mouth to speak, and found the words dried up in his throat.

The man smiled again, making Precious shudder. "Ah, I see you remember me. Good. Nice little trick, using your dogs to try and remove me." The man leant back, one leg over the other, and flicked through the small bookcase build into the wall. "Still, they gave me a fright. Caught me off my guard, you may say. Nearly blew everything. Thing is about my old job, which I'm sure is now mine again, is you learn not only the unpleasant people, but what motivates them. Not really any difference to yourself, it's money of course."

Precious watched in terror. The thing in his back felt like a blade, maybe just a knife, but if pressed any harder it would cut through his robes and into his back. The holder seemed to know how much pressure he needed. The visitor with the squeaky voice thumbed absently through a tattered old book, then replaced it, upside down.

"Funny thing too about all my finances. 'Obtained for the benefit of the city' I was told when I made some passive enquiries. Sure that was a mistake, agreed?"

Precious nodded as enthusiastically as he could without moving. The man smiled his horrid smile and looked through another book.

"Glad to see we agree. Now, here's what you are going to do." He put the book back upside down, stood, and arranged his black robe so it fell neatly. "Firstly you will restore all my previous possessions, finances and position, secondly you will declare your dogs criminals, death upon their return to the city, but neglect to announce it until they return. Finally," the man squeaked, leaning close to the mayor, watching the flesh of his podgy cheeks ripple with fear. "Finally," he repeated, distracted, "you will resign from office, into my personal care. Your last act will be to transfer all business to me. Understand?"

Precious nodded, tears flowing slowly. The pressure in his back held steady.

"You will arrange it all right now, and no tricks or scams, or else." The man glanced to his accomplice and a small prick of fire coursed into the mayors back as the knife briefly darted into the soft tissue, making him yelp in shock and pain, the blade gone as fast as it had come. It moved a few centimetres up and held there again. "Do you understand?"

Precious nodded, feeling his hands shaking on the polished desk.

The man smiled again and returned to the chair, selecting another book. "Begin," he said with a vague wave of his free hand. Precious took his first sheet in hands like grass in a gale and tried to insert the quill into the inkwell. On the third attempt he managed it. "By the way," the man said as Precious was about to put pen to paper, "Parks has only one 'P' and one 'S'."

Chris watched the old man closely as he tipped some steaming water from the blackened pot over the camp fire. In the flickering light John sat in revered silence of the man he knew by legend. The old man's companion sat leant against a tree stump, a tired expression on his aged face. Marty lay on the flat bonnet of the car, rifle in his arms.

"My name is Guy O'Brian," said the old man, sniffing the dented metal mugs, and taking a cautious sip. "I have been very lucky, I guess. I found some old books in the woods, hidden in a haunted house. I saved them, battered but readable, and taught myself to read." Chris nodded patiently. Marty looked up from his stargazing, then look back into the cosmos. "I found they were books on electricity, what it does, what it is, and how to use it. My father was livid I had spent so long trying to learn. He was a fisherman, like most here. I said I could help him get more fish, I even designed a huge boat to collect fish. He didn't like it."

"He hated it," said the other man. "Ian Halford," he offered, then returned to brooding silence.

"My half brother," Guy explained. "He helped me a lot when I was young, but not so much now. I fear I have used him up." Guy smiled. Ian did not.

"So you can repair the city's power system?" Chris asked.

"Sure," said Guy. I can sort most power systems, even some back there," he waved at the town. "But they didn't seem too interested in my designs to improve everything. They even laughed when I said I could turn sunlight into electricity."

"They were going to burn you as a wizard," muttered Ian, not looking up from the fire.

"True," said Guy, the ghost of a smile saved for old memories. "Now I just tinker. My cart those scoundrels turned over was filled with the things I had made. Little trinkets that made a noise, or lit up. I sold them for children, kept me alive and fed. A lot went over the water."

"There's something past that massive puddle?" asked Marty, sitting up.

"Yeah," said Ian, "a load of diseases, people to kill you and more of those things that attacked us."

Chris gave Ian a passive look then touched Guy's torn sleeve. "Can you come with us? The mayor promised us he would employ you at a handsome rate."

John nodded. "It's true. I'm his Attendant and an inventor too. He said you can have your own office, budget and authority."

Guy looked into the flames, searching for his answer in the embers.

"I think," he said finally, "that would be interesting. What is the system for, and why do you need it?"

"It runs the under the surface transport, lighting, and visual boxes so we can see where we aren't," said Chris. "We need it to remove a pest infestation."

Guy looked at Marty's rifle. "A lot of pests?"

"Big pests with teeth, brains and appetite," said Chris.

Ian snorted in irritation and stretched his legs closer to the heat. As the sun had set the temperature had dropped rapidly. They could now see their breath in the light of the fire. Chris ignored Ian and took the mug offered by Guy.

"Thanks. You say you taught yourself to read?"

"Not easy," said Guy, "but I did it."

"I know. I did the same," said Chris, passing the mug to John.

Guy fixed his eyes to Chris for longer then he needed. The mutual respect grew between the two men.

"So now what?" grumbled Ian, ignoring the mug offered by John.

"Now, dear half brother," Guy said, "we go to their big city, fix their problems, and live easy."

Ian grunted again, expressing his feelings of easy living.

In the storehouse Piers felt a little anxious. Chris and the others had been gone a long time, and the men were getting restless. They were training as hard as they could, still doing regular patrols, and checking traps laid in busy areas. But no matter the workload the fact their leader was absent made them feel complacent. Three fights over petty things had already broken out, quickly quashed. One man had vanished for over an hour, only to be found with a young lady nearby. Piers felt his control slipping, and tried to imitate Chris, but the more he tried, the more they rebelled, and the worse he felt. Failure seemed imminent, the group would fall apart and Chris would dispose of him from his position, a failed leader.

The noise in the open interior nearly drowned the thud on the heavy door. Piers was close by, feeling safer by the exit. He slid back the lock and looked out. The guard was lying on the floor, a small trickle of blood from his brow. Piers opened his mouth to shout a warning, then all went black.

Chapter Twenty-Four

The dull patchy walls loomed high above them as the Land Rover bounced over the rough roads to the east gate. Guy had been once years before, but Ian hadn't, and both men were awed by the sheer, flat cliff that rose above them. The buttress shrouding the gate looked like a mouse hole in a wall, small and dark and forbidding. Chris ignored the view, concentrating on finding the smoothest path around the broken road surface. He had a niggle in his head, a sense finely attuned to danger, that was warning him. He nudged Marty, and motioned to the gun mounted in front of the passenger seat. Marty looked puzzled, then caught the look and checked the weapon was loaded and ready. John saw the movement and copied, even though he knew little on the big gun mounted on the back.

Chris slowed as he neared the gate, waiting for the challenge from the walls. To his surprise the gates opened without a word said. John smiled, relieved their return was pre-empted. Chris felt even more nervous. Once inside the thick steel braced wooden gates clanged shut. There was nobody there, or anywhere. The streets were deserted. Chris stopped at the edge of the holding area, the gate into the city open like a toothless mouth. Motioning to John to get in the drivers seat Chris pulled his rifle from the holder on the side, and without looking moved forwards, rifle to his shoulder, half bent over. Marty copied him. John ground the gears briefly, making Chris cringe, then followed slowly. Guy and Ian kept silent, sensing something was about to happen, and unsure what to do about it.

Moving as a pair, each covering the other, Chris and Marty moved from street corner to street corner, checking each junction before moving on. Still the streets were empty, no sign of anyone anywhere. Sweat dripped from the armed men's faces as they concentrated fully searching for danger. Chris led them slowly towards the storehouse, knowing he had to check his men first. As the entered the road that passed it, there was still nothing, but Chris felt his instinct warning him. With a subtle hand gesture he told Marty to stay, Marty crouched down and covered the area staring down the black barrel of his rifle. Almost stooping like an old man Chris stepped slowly and deliberately along the side of a storehouse. He could see theirs ahead, on the slight curve in the road as it followed the river. There was no sign of damage, or a fight, but a dark stain on the pale road could have been blood. Still moving slowly forwards Chris scanned the road, the walls, the rooftops for people, explosives, anything unusual. Still seeing nothing he waved Marty and the car to follow.

As they neared the storehouse the small door opened. Chris and Marty instantly dropped to one knee, weapons raised. John stalled the car stopping behind them. Feeling vulnerable John pulled a pistol from a holster in the dash and tried to cock it. A small, robed figure stepped into the growing shadow from the afternoon sun, an oversized hood hiding their face. Chris and Marty didn't move.

"Welcome back, Mr Spencer," said the robe in a squeaky voice. The figure flipped back the hood in one fluid gesture.

"Well, well," said Chris, still knelt, "Agent Parks.

Wondered what had happened to you."

Parks laughed, a shrill childlike noise. "Well, wonder no more great white Hunter, for here I am. You nearly ruined me, but I do not give in so easily. Like you, I am a fighter, only I fight for what I want, what I need, not to help random strangers, but we do both have some sort of a reputation."

Chris didn't smile. With professional precision he flicked the safety off his rifle, and fired two shots into the road by the small man's feet. He was rewarded with the shocked recoil of the agent as he leapt back from the sound and impacts.

"Indeed," Parks said when he had regained his composure. "Like that is it?" Parks smiled again, still red faced from shock, and straightened his robes.

"It it," said Chris through clenched teeth. "Now tell me why I shouldn't plug you right now?"

"Because, Hunter, you want your team, your things and your equipment. They are all in here, but to get them you have to get by me, and my men." Parks paused as the street, the storehouse roof and the roof opposite filled with men, armed with Chris' own rifles from the armoury. "If you want them, come and get them." Parks smiled his evil smile. "Payback time, Spencer. If you don't get in, they die. Good luck." Parks flipped his hood back up, and walked back inside. As the door slammed shut Chris quickly counted the opposing force.

A quick head count made over thirty, but most would be unused to projectile weaponry. Also none had their level of experience and skill. Still, with that much aimed at the two men, it would be hard to get out of it unscathed. Looking back Chris saw two large carts blocking the road, pushed there quietly while he had spoken to Parks.

Silence hung like fog in the street. Nobody moved, nobody made the first move. Chris and Marty held their positions, Chris ten feet from the car, Marty five on the other side. The pistol in John's hand shook slightly as he willed his hand to still. The men in the road, and those on the rooftops looked uncertainly from each other to the to men below. The side door flew open and Parks, his hood still up, put his head out briefly.

"Kill them, you fools!" he shrieked, them slammed the door back. Guns clicked as safety catches were turned to off.

"Marty," said Chris quietly.

"Yeah, boss?" There was no sign of nervousness, Chris noted, just anticipation.

"You go right roof, I go left roof, then take the guys below. Guy, Ian? Keep your heads down. When you get a chance hide away from the car, in case they have anything stronger. John, keep your head down, but be ready to drive."

John leant forwards and touched the key hanging from the ignition, gently holding it between finger and thumb. Guy and Ian tried to hide in the exposed rear tub of the car, Marty cocked his head from left to right slowly, with a horrid crack of neck bones. Chris closed his eyes, took a deep breath, and screamed.

Chapter Twenty-Five

From the first yell from Chris both he and Marty sprang forwards, taking aimed deliberate shots. By the time they had moved forwards ten feet, five bodies had fallen from the rooftops, another two were down on the roofs, and one was screaming sickeningly. Pausing to reload, without knowing how many rounds were left, stone chips flew around them as badly aimed shots hit walls, the floor, everywhere but their targets. As Chris expected they were aiming fast, hoping to hit something. With fresh magazines in they pressed their backs against the walls, aiming at the opposite side, picking off targets one by one, haloed by dust and cordite smoke. Barely twenty seconds from the start half of Park's men were down, either dead or wounded. Chris had a graze on his leg from a lucky shot, Marty had cuts to his face from stone chips. John slid down so he was hidden by the dash of the car, and fired his pistol. A few shots hit the car, making a noise of rocks thrown onto a metal door.

Chris reloaded, shouting 'reloading' so Marty knew he wasn't hurt, or unable to fight. Marty did the same when he hit empty. Spent cases bounced from above, rolling around on the floor like hail. Chris knew the men by the door were still a threat, but he had to clear the high ground first. With his eyes stinging from the smoke, and ears ringing he fired, aimed, fired, aimed, until he became numb to the world, only his rifle and the target existed.

A scream of pain cut him from his withdrawal. He looked down to see Marty was on the ground, blood soaking his shirt. Sudden rage welled up, an anger without definition, without control. He saw the pained, almost apologetic look on the young man's face as he tried with limp hands to grasp his rifle. Another round hit his shoulder, spinning him around. Chris saw no more. Sliding a fresh magazine in he stood, flicked the control switch to semi and sprayed rounds first against the wall before him, before stepping forwards to do the same to the other wall. He walked backwards, pumping the trigger to keep the three round bursts going. After ten pulls the bolt stayed back, as the magazine was empty. He reloaded without looking, dropping the magazine to the floor, flipped the release catch and fired again. The shot that hit him took him completely by surprise.

Hitting his left arm, deflecting from his elbow and into his side he first staggered, then dropped to one knee. Disbelieving the blood that dripped to the floor, his blood, he stood, but his left arm was numb, useless. Dropping the rifle he drew his pistol, awkward from the holster on his right hip, being left handed he struggled to aim, when another shot hit his right shin, taking his feet from under him. As he landed, facing the car, he saw John leap from his seat and run towards him, wildly firing his pistol. The aim of the few defenders changed and John slid to a stop a few feet short, motionless. Still shocked Chris rolled back to Marty, the young man pale and crying. He reached out with his right hand to Marty, seeing the shadow of an armed man fall over them both. Looking up he saw the barrel of one of his rifles staring back. The anger still held and Chris snarled defiance at the grime smeared face behind the gun. He heard the boom of a gun, flinching involuntarily, realising he was still alive. The man had vanished. More shots, these heavier than the ones from before, echoed down the close confines of the street. Chunks of stonework the size of fists fell from the walls, men screaming and trying to run. More shots, deep booming shots, chased them, one man was cut in two as he tried to run. When the dust and smoke had cleared only bodies lay on the red soaked ground.

Chris tried to sit up, failed and rolled over instead. Past John's still body he saw Guy sat behind the small machine gun on the car, and Ian behind the big gun. Both men swung their guns slowly around, checking for anyone left. Chris tried again to stand, feeling sick and dizzy. His left arm hung by his side, painless but tingling. He hopped on his left leg, ignoring the damage he could be doing, over to the car. Without a word he pulled a green plastic box from the back and tore open a bandage pack.

"You ok?" asked Ian, still sat behind the big gun.

Chris shook his head, and tried to bandage his arm one handed. Guy slid over to Chris can helped, firstly with his arm, then his leg. Using Guy as a crutch Chris went to check John, then Marty. John was dead, a shot through his neck had cut his throat and spine cleanly. With stinging eyes Chris closed the Attendants eyelids. Marty was bad. One shot to his stomach, another to his hip. They bandaged him up, then Chris hobbled to the metal door.

Inside his men were all tied up, hooded and subdued. There was nobody else left. Cursing Chris released the first man, telling him to free the others, then ordered someone to take him and Marty to the medical rooms. Once in the back of another Land Rover Chris closed his eyes and drifted away.

He woke to warm sheets, soft voices, chemical smells

and pain. He opened his eyes, strained in the light, and tried to focus.

"Ah, the man returns," said a friendly voice. "Thought you were gone. Lucky you made it."

"Who are you?" Chris asked, feeling stupid.

"You medic," the man said. As his vision cleared Chris saw he was in a small room, on a metal framed bed. Some sort of bag was hanging beside him, feeing a thin tube plugged into his arm. The bag was full of red fluid. "You lost a lot of blood," said the medic, following his gaze. "Close to losing too much."

Chris then checked his left arm. It was held in what looked like stone, immobile, but his fingers moved. As did his right toes, his right leg also in stone. His tattered clothes were replaced with a white gown, and he felt cleaner, so somebody must have bathed him. He felt a flush of shame warm his cheeks.

"You leg was broken, quite badly, but we fixed it. Same with your arm. Got the bullet out of your side too. A couple of months and you'll be up and about again." The medic smiled warmly, and left.

"You had better, you lazy bugger. Can't stand your snoring," said a familiar voice. Wheeling himself in on a wheeled chair Marty smiled. "Can hear you down the hallway, like a saw cutting hard wood."

Chris didn't speak, he couldn't stop the tears, fresh and open, that poured down his cheeks. Holding his right hand out he reached for Marty, who came closer and they grasped each others hands firmly, Marty joining in until they both cried like children.

"Hell of a day?" said Marty when they had calmed down.

"Hell of a day," agreed Chris. "Poor John."

"Yeah, poor sod. They got Parks."

"Did they?"

"Yep," Marty nodded. "Found him, well, most of him. Looks like the underworld he was working with caught up with him. Chopped him into chunks and spread him all over."

"Good," said Chris.

"Also, Guy had fixed the power, so Piers and the guys have cleared the tunnels, and even got the transport working."

"Bloody hell! How long have I been out?"

Marty looked away. "A month."

"Bloody hell," Chris repeated.

"Anyway, I'm off. Found a nice nurse who wants to

give me a bath. Don't want to upset her. Cheer up, you old bugger. We made it." Marty gave his hand one more squeeze and reversed out the room. Lingering at the door he took in the sight of the man he had known all his memorable life lying helpless, in casts, on a bed. Marty would be longer before he was recovered, but he knew they could return to their old life. But would they want to? With a smile he didn't feel Marty waved and wheeled himself away.

Chris lay back and stared at the ceiling. His left arm felt like fire, his right leg itched, and he was terribly hungry. But he was alive, and so was Marty. He cried, not only over John, but with joy over their survival.

Chapter Twenty-Six

The following spring the infestation was removed, lights blazed brightly throughout the city and a parade wound it's lazy way around the wide main streets. Following the token lead of one squad of City Law men came the mayoral buggy, with a large platform on the rear where the returned mayor Precious sat waving happily to the crowds. Then came the marching men of the new City Security, armed with rifles and wearing camouflage. At the rear, in a bullet ridden and smoking Land Rover came Chris and Marty, not waving, not smiling, just keeping a professional air. As they neared the west gate the procession stopped, the Security men, lead by Piers, parted and formed four ranks, two either side, facing in. Chris drove past them, stopping behind the mayors buggy. Precious turned his chair around and spoke loudly to the crowd.

"Today we say farewell to the men who saved us, not only from the pest menace, not only from a corrupt and now removed organisation, but also from years of poor production. Today the first electricity machines run, powering our new future. I say to these men," Precious held his hands to Chris and Marty, "I say thank you, and good luck. There is always a place here for you, should you need it."

The crowds cheered, slapping hands and stamping their feet. Chris waved briefly, Marty more enthusiastically. The crowds parted, opening the way to the west gate, with stood wide and clear, showing the plains beyond. Chris coaxed the ailing car forwards and out the gates, picking up speed. As they cleared the outer gate and into the cool morning light the smells of grass, animal dung, pollen and dirt filled their noses.

Marty whooped loudly, leaning back almost to the point of falling out. He noticed in the back something he had missed. Two large wooden crates under some old tarpuline.

"What's that?" he asked Chris.

"What?" he answered, not looking back.

"Those boxes," Marty said, feeling irritated. He started to climb into the back, but Chris grabbed his ankle, stopping him.

"It's our reward," he said.

"Reward?" asked Marty, sitting back down.

"Well, never work for free." Chris said, plain faced. Marty went for the boxes again and Chris didn't stop him. They were about two feet square, with rope handles on two sides. Pulling the thick lid off the first Marty saw gold, lots of gold. They were coins mostly, all different sizes, some bits of jewellery and decorative trinkets. In the other was more coins, and a thick paper envelope. Holding carefully to the paper in case it blew away in the open car Marty pulled out two pieces of clean white paper from the envelope and read them. Shock, surprise, and then joy showed on his young face.

"You knew about this?" he demanded of Chris, waving the paper in his face.

"I think we earned it," Chris said.

Marty put the paper back into the envelope with surgical care, then closed up the boxes, checking the lids were firm. Back in the front he looked at Chris, the growing grey in the older man's hair, the deepening creases in his face. Every man needed a retirement plan,

Chris had said. Clever bugger, Marty thought. Clever, clever bugger.

As they sped away from the city, back of the smoking Land Rover sagging under the weight of gold, and two very special pieces of paper worth far more, Marty started to laugh. The air was clear, the dust of inactivity blowing away. They were off to new adventures.

In the drivers seat Chris finally smiled. He was home.

Printed in Great Britain
by Amazon